THE LINEUP

LON BRADEN. They all heard his threat the night the news shark was killed . . . and Braden took the rap.

PAUL SAVAGE. TV was his business, power was his passion. And everyone wanted him—dead.

ANNE GRONOUSKI. Assistant D.A. It's her first big case, the one that can land her in clover . . . or have her pushing up daisies.

CLINT TOLLIVER. The Godfather, Texas style, only backs winners—and he's just put his money on Hellinger.

BILL ROSSETTI. The Government's secret link to the Braden case. He's playing with dynamite . . . and Hellinger's holding the lighted fuse.

HELLINGER'S LAW

IT'S OFF THE RECORD—AND ON THE LINE.

HELLINGER'S LAW
THE GOOD OF THE PEOPLE

A NOVEL BY JUSTIN BARR
BASED ON THE UNIVERSAL TELEVISION PRODUCTION
TELEPLAY BY LAWRENCE VAIL AND JACK LAIRD
STORY BY TED LEIGHTON & LAWRENCE VAIL

A JOVE BOOK

Copyright © 1980 by MCA Publishing, a Division of MCA Inc.

All rights reserved. No part of this publication may be reproduced or transmitted in any form or by any means, electronic or mechanical, including photocopy, recording, or any information storage and retrieval system, without permission in writing from the publisher.

Requests for permission to make copies of any part of the work should be mailed to: Permissions, Jove Publications, Inc., 200 Madison Avenue, New York, NY 10016

First Jove edition published December 1980

10 9 8 7 6 5 4 3 2 1

Printed in the United States of America

Jove books are published by Jove Publications, Inc., 200 Madison Avenue, New York, NY 10016

HELLINGER'S LAW

CHAPTER 1

NICK HELLINGER stretched his broad, naked back and ran a hand over his shaved head. He bent down over his pin striped pants to tie his black shoes. Then he sighed and rose from the edge of the bed and gazed out the large window over the Philadelphia skyline. He had long ago decided that it was not a better city just because he practiced law in it, and decided he didn't care. Most mornings it was all he could do to care about his current case, whatever it was, without considering grander matters.

His apartment was sparsely but expensively furnished. On the walls were framed diplomas and photographs of Hellinger with some of his more famous clients—Congressmen and show-business personalities.

But when he moved through the apartment, his bearing suggested a man with scant interest in his immediate personal environment. He was tall, with a certain lusty roughness in his mannerisms; his face was strong, with an aquiline nose, dark eyes, sensuous mouth. He shoved aside a chair with his knee and stood close to the window, feeling the morning sun slanting in on him as he stretched. He snatched his striped shirt from where it had been flung over the back of the sofa and worked his arms and shoulders into it.

He gazed at the distant statue of William Penn atop City Hall and sighed again.

"Well, Brotherly Love," he muttered, "smile on me today and we'll beat a murder rap. And with luck, I won't even be held in contempt."

He snorted with a contempt of his own. The law was the law. It would be a rough day, but in his hands, the law was closer to *his* law. Sometimes his ability to manipulate people and situations made him uncomfortable. But this client was innocent, and he felt a bit of sympathy for the assistant DA, a nice young kid named Alan Handler. If Handler learned enough from what he would be put through in court today, he would get some place. Rather him than Bernie Nussbaum, the DA, who was a much tougher infighter and who could make things a lot more difficult for Hellinger's client.

The phone rang, he picked it up without saying anything.

"Your car's ready, Mr. Hellinger," came the voice.

"Yeah."

He took his topcoat and hat out of the closet. He didn't like topcoats, but he loved autumn. And every couple of years or so even took a long enough vacation to enjoy the fall season. By Christmas, maybe, this year. Unless he lost this case, in which event it would be back to his books to prepare for an appeal, which would push back his vacation. But he definitely was getting tired and needed some time off, time away from everything.

"Hey, Hellinger," he said aloud to himself as he pushed the elevator button, "cut out the whining."

It was hot in Houston. Lon Braden was sweating behind the wheel, even with the air conditioning on. He shot through three red lights, wheeled onto the approach ramp, and barged into the freeway traffic, narrowly missing a semi whose air-horn resounded in his station wagon.

Under ordinary circumstances, he was the most careful and calculating of men, as might be expected of an accountant. But now his life was a high-wire walk, and somebody had sabotaged the rigging. People would kill for numbers and names.

There were 86,400 seconds in a day; less than 14,000 were left before the ten-o'clock news. The countdown continued with cruel persistence as he fought his way through rush-hour traffic to put the buildings of downtown Houston behind him.

The years had taught him that his nerves were good. In his position, a less courageous man might have just kept on running, but by his calculations there was still time, still a chance. He took his obligations seriously.

Exiting at the Astrodome, he spotted the cluster of yellow schoolbuses at the far end of the vast, otherwise empty parking lot and, without slowing, aimed the station wagon for them. He wasn't aware of how fast he was going until he hit the brakes. The wagon fishtailed, slid sideways, and spun, finally coming to a hot halt. He jumped out and ran toward the open gate.

Inside the Astrodome, dwarfed by the huge, nearly empty arena, a high-school band high-stepped down the center of the artificial turf of the football field, playing a spirited march. Nearer to a section of the lowest seats where a group of mothers watched, a unit of elementary-school baton twirlers, in sequined blue tights and silver vests, went through their routine.

Braden burst from the tunnel onto the field, then abruptly slowed and assumed as deliberate and calm an attitude as possible. He was able to pick out his daughter, Julie, among the twirlers—she was the smallest and wore large glasses.

He straightened his tie and smoothed his jacket as he walked toward them around the base of the stands. As he got nearer, he could hear the voice of the instructor of the twirlers giving commands:

"Twirl . . . throw . . . catch . . . turn . . . that's it . . ."

He searched the group of mothers for his wife. She saw him first, stood, and waved to him. He quickened his pace, trying to be unobtrusive when he passed the children, but knowing Julie would see him.

His wife kept her eyes on him, she knew something was up. He motioned casually for her to come over to him.

"Good, girls . . . " the instructor encouraged, "good! Turn and strut—one, two, three, four . . . twirl . . ."

"Lon, what's the matter?"

Braden waited until his wife was close to him, then said in a low voice, trying to appear casual, "I'll explain it all later, Cara. I'm in a hurry." He pressed the car keys into her hand. "I want you to take the wagon home."

"But you look so upset. What is it, Lon?"

"Just listen closely. And try not to seem upset yourself, okay?"

"But, darling . . . why should I take the wagon? What is going on—"

"*Please*, Cara." He flashed a wide smile, for the benefit of anybody who might be watching. "I'm running out of time. Don't make a big deal out of it. Just do exactly what I tell you."

"Something at work, isn't it?"

It was difficult to maintain the smile. "Cara."

"Okay, okay."

"Soon as they're finished rehearsing the number"— he nodded toward the twirlers—"grab Julie and head for home. Pack a couple of bags, then sit by the phone till you hear from me."

"Pack! Lon, what will you do?"

"I'll grab a cab. I have to stop a couple of places, then I'll be home. I'll let you know."

"Lon, you're scared of something. You're scaring me. What's—"

He put his fingers to her lips in an affectionate gesture, quieting her. "I'm not afraid, just in a hurry. Don't you be frightened, just do what I say. Don't leave the house. Don't let Julie use the phone. And if anybody else calls, get them off the line quick. Keep it open. I'll call." He pulled her head down and kissed her forehead. "Love you."

"Something to do with Trans-Tex, right?" Her voice quavered.

"Tell you later. Now, smile, and go on back. Anybody asks, say I just dropped off the car so you could run a couple of errands. Tell Julie we're going on a trip. And for chrissake, try and look normal!"

He tossed Julie a wave, and headed for the exit.

Braden was expert at organization. He had called ahead for a cab to pick him up, and there it was, waiting for him. And he had had the foresight to tell the dispatcher his destination and need for speed, so the driver could have already thought out the quickest route.

Still, it was growing dark when they arrived at the TV studio. Braden hurried in.

Lights glared, cameras were being moved around, people scampered this way and that arranging things, calling directions, writing on clipboards. The set for the news broadcast was familiar, the people sitting behind the broadcasters' desks were not. Apparently they were just stand-ins to help set the camera angles and so forth.

A man directed, "Move in tight on George, camera one... good... Two, pick up Adrian... Okay, George, look over at three now... Come in tighter, three..."

The rear wall of the set bore the customary large black-and-white portrait with the logo beside it: WATCHDOG with PAUL SAVAGE. Excellent likeness—Braden thought—captures the meanness.

He grabbed a passing woman's elbow. "Where's Savage?" he barked.

"Oh, Mr. Braden." Recognition, no smile.

"Where's Savage?"

"He's not here."

"Know where he is?"

She shook her head. "I'm sorry." She started away.

"Hey, don't walk off!"

"Would you please let go of my arm?"

"Sorry." Braden dropped his hand. "But I have to find him."

"I wish I could help you."

"What's your name, may I ask?"

"Laura." She cocked her head.

He had attracted the attention of the crew now, and regretted that. He moved closer to her and lowered his voice. "Well, look, Laura, I have to find him. He won't return my calls. I have to talk to him *now*, before the broadcast."

"We have a policy—"

"I don't care about your damn policy!"

"What's going on over there?" called the director. "Who is that guy?" He started toward them.

Braden gritted his teeth. "I'm warning you, Laura, your boss is headed for a million-dollar lawsuit—if I don't strangle him first."

Her hand nervously clutched at her neck. "I tell you, he's not here. That's all I know."

"Mister"—the director sighed with exasperation—"we're trying to set up here."

"Fine." Braden put his hands on his hips. "Just tell me where I can find Paul Savage."

"He doesn't even leave home until eight. And when he gets here, he doesn't have time to—"

"He's still *home?*"

Laura piped up quickly, "We don't actually know where he is . . ."

But Braden was already trotting for the door.

"Dumb broad," Braden muttered to himself in the back of the taxi. "Knows enough to know me, then plays stupid."

Among the many bits of private information about the area that Braden was privileged to know was where Paul Savage lived. Savage was a secretive bastard who covered up his tracks with all kinds of ruses, falsehoods, guises. Unlisted this, unregistered that. All part of his act—didn't he think people could find out? Dangerous, unprincipled rotter who came out of hiding only to ruin people's lives. Half the time he didn't even know whom or what he was hurting.

The cab reached an elegant section of snobbishly secluded homes on the outskirts of town. But right ahead, a white Cadillac Fleetwood, its top visible above the low wall that surrounded Savage's property.

Braden had the cab continue on a couple of hundred yards. He paid the driver and waited for the cab to leave before turning back to Savage's house.

"Look, buster," Paul Savage was saying to the hulking, stoop-shouldered man in Savage's study, "it's a little late in the game for you to hustle me." Savage, nearing fifty, had a large head with thick, curly hair atop narrow shoulders and a small body. He looked bigger and better on TV.

"I need more," the man said, "that's the simple fact. And I'm worth it, to you." The man squirmed in his chair, which was near Savage's and for a few seconds avoided the broadcaster's eyes.

It was an intimate setting—desk on which was a small television, fireplace, walls lined with bookshelves, large reel-to-reel tape recorder standing on the floor, the scene lit by a single table lamp next to Savage. The phone on his desk was off the hook. Through the open French doors came the sound of the lawn sprinklers.

"You get into debt with the loan sharks, don't come crying to me," Savage said. "You get what I think you're worth. Don't push me."

"Suppose I suddenly didn't have any more information for you."

A thin smile appeared on Savage's lips. "Suppose

you listen to a little something." Keeping his eyes on the man, Savage reached over and switched on the tape machine. The first voice was his own:

Let's talk about pornography.

The man sat up straight. The next voice was his, and his shock was obvious.

Yeah, right. The mob's got a lock on it in Houston, like I told you. There ain't a skin flick or snuff film around without the mob's price tag on it. I'll name a couple of names, but look, Paul, we gotta talk about money. I'm into these guys deep, and I gotta raise my prices. You want what I got, you're gonna have to pay—

The man lurched forward and violently switched off the machine.

"You recorded me," he snarled. "You son of a bitch." He remained leaning forward, fists on his knees, eyes burning at Savage. "You dumb son of a bitch."

The menacing look caused Savage to flinch, but he kept his voice cool, gave a quick wave of the hand. "Not dumb, cautious. You were dumb not to think I'd be cautious."

"It ain't cautious to double-cross me, you punk. I'll take the tape."

He reached, Savage pushed his arm away from the machine, saying, "Relax! The tape was made for me only, for my private files. I'd never use it."

"Hell you wouldn't!" The man jumped up and smacked Savage with the back of his hand, sending the broadcaster sprawling out of his chair beside the desk. Feeling behind himself, the man wrapped his big hand around the fireplace poker.

Savage sat up facing him, shakily holding a .32 automatic. "Hold it right there!" Keeping both hands on the gun, he clumsily got up. "Right where you are!"

"Or you'll what?" The sneering man chuckled, baring his teeth, and took another step. "You plan to use that toy, Savage, you better slip the safety off."

Savage glanced down, the man swung the poker. It cracked a deep crease in Savage's head, which quickly welled with blood. Savage toppled over, falling against the table and bringing down the lamp whose globe splattered on the floor.

"Dumb goddamned punk," the man muttered as he yanked out his handkerchief to wipe his prints from the poker.

The doorbell rang. The man instinctively crouched in the darkened room. The bell rang again, and a voice called, "Savage? Savage! I know you're in there!"

As the bell rang a third time, the man groped for the tape recorder. His big hands felt roughly around for the tape. His wrist hit the switch, the machine went on. "Shit." He got his hands on the spinning reels, ripped both of them off the machine.

Tucking the reels under his arm, he bolted through the French doors and across the rear yard, his trousers whipping through the spray from the sprinklers. He reached the wall, planted his free hand on the top, and vaulted over.

Slowly, quietly, he picked his way around the outside of the wall toward the front of the house. There was no one at the door. Whoever had rung the doorbell was either inside the house or gone.

The man headed off parallel to the street, staying behind the shrubbery.

When Braden left the cab, his fondest hope was that Savage would be reasonable. Braden would seem both ominous and honest, tell him that there were things he couldn't know about this matter, things that were terribly important. And he would use the old ploy: in exchange for holding off on the story for now, Braden would give him the whole, real, *sensational* story later, when he could.

And if that didn't work—well, maybe he'd pull the sparkplugs on that damned Fleetwood.

But the fact was, Braden was scared to death to confront Paul Savage. Because he'd have to stop the man from making that broadcast, no matter what. And for an essentially nonviolent man, the available choices of means for doing that—should Savage not be reasonable—were scary.

He walked up the driveway toward the house. There was only one light on in a first-floor room. He thought he heard angry voices. Just before he reached the front door, that light went off.

Either Savage had seen him approaching, or he was preparing to leave.

Braden rang the bell.

The house was quiet. There was no time for games.

"Savage?" Braden called. "Savage! I know you're in there!"

He rang the bell again, and a third time, leaning on it.

It occurred to him that Savage might be sneaking

out another way. Well, the bastard would have to come around to his Cadillac sooner or later.

Or would he? Maybe he had another car somewhere, or somebody picking him up around the corner.

Braden had to take the offense. He tried the door, it was locked. Keeping an eye on the front, he began working his way around the dark house. When he came to the rear, first he heard the revolving sprinklers. Then he saw the moonlight glint off the open French doors.

"Savage!" The creep had left through the back. And left the doors open behind him? Braden sloshed through the sprinklers and peered cautiously in. "Savage?"

He stepped inside. He could barely make out anything. There was a whirring sound, a hum, like maybe a small fan left on. He stumbled over something and almost cried out.

What he had stumbled over was a foot. He could see the body dimly outlined. His eyes adjusted. There was just enough moonlight. Broken lamp beside a bloody face. He knelt beside the face.

Savage! Just beyond his outstretched right arm, a pistol.

Braden was squeamish. But the scene also numbed him. He put two fingers to the man's jugular. Nothing. Savage was dead. Shot, maybe, with that gun.

No. Whatever had happened had happened just as Braden was arriving, because he heard voices, and the light went out. He had heard no shot.

The he saw the poker. He knew he mustn't touch it. Mustn't touch anything.

There would be a phone on the desk. Braden felt for it, his eyes still on dead Paul Savage. So there would be no broadcast, that problem was solved. Might as well tip the cops before getting out of there. He found the phone, the receiver was off the hook. He would wipe it off after making the call.

Suddenly the howl of an approaching siren rent the night. Braden froze. Coming closer. He dashed into the hall to the front window.

A black-and-white squad car screeched to a halt in the driveway behind the Cadillac. Two cops leaped out.

Braden didn't dare get tied into this, not even for questioning. He darted back to the study and out the French doors. He tripped over a sprinkler and slid headlong on the soppy grass. He scrambled to his feet.

"Freeze! Police!"

A bright flashlight beam blinded him.

"Move, you're a dead man!"

The second officer moved through the flashlight beam, gun drawn. "I'll cover him here," the cop said. "Dockery, you better check inside.

Cara Braden, dressed in a happy-blue pants suit but not at all happy, sat tensely by the phone. She brushed imagined lint off her legs, looked at her lacquered nails.

Julie, in jeans and a pullover sweater, sat cross-legged in the center of the room near the three packed suitcases. She sifted through some record albums. "When will he call, Mommy?"

"When he can," she snapped.

Julie slid a record out of its envelope and put it on the stereo. Music of the Bee Gees invaded the room.

"Julie!"

"What?" Julie blinked innocently.

"Not now!"

"No music? But it's so *boring* just waiting."

"Okay, I know." Cara shook her head apologetically and went over to the turntable. "I'm sorry. Just a little nervous. We'll turn it down a little, okay?"

"Sure. Why are you nervous?"

"You know, when you're waiting for something."

The phone rang, Cara sprang to answer it, covering her other ear with her hand. "Hello?"

"Hi, honey."

"Lon! It's about time! Where are you?"

"Listen closely, and don't get excited or worried. I've been . . . detained. At the police station. Now just listen, it's going to be okay."

"What happened? Lon, what happened?"

"No big deal. Just a screwup. I'll tell you about it later. But right now I want you to call the company. They will tell you exactly what to do."

"The company! I knew Trans-Tex had something to do with this!"

"Well, you're wrong. Except that they want to take care of me, make sure everything's straightened out."

"So we're not going anywhere?"

"Well, maybe you are. Don't ask me questions now, okay? I have to get off the phone. Just call them. Do what they say. They'll explain things. And we'll talk later."

"You're not, not in *jail?*"

"Well . . ."

"Oh, God, Lon!"

"I'm fine. And I'm depending on you. They'll take care of everything."

"Yeah, just like always."

"Hey! They're doing it for me, okay?"

"Okay."

"Do exactly what they say."

CHAPTER 2

THE UNIFORMED bus driver leaned forward in the witness chair, cleared his throat, and flicked his finger in the direction of the dark-haired man sitting at the defense table next to Nick Hellinger. "That's the man who boarded my bus—right over there."

The assistant district attorney turned in the same direction and nodded. "Let the record show that the witness has identified the defendant, James Camilli." He turned back to the witness. "At what time of night was that?"

"Objection," Nick said casually. "He wants it to be night, Your Honor, let him establish it."

"Strike the question," the prosecutor said, letting his eyes fall shut for an instant. "At what *time* was that?"

"I always hit that corner between eleven-oh-two and eleven-oh-six p.m.," the bus driver said. "That was when it was."

The prosecutor faced the jury. "So that puts the defendant within three blocks of the murder site mere minutes after the crime was committed." He smiled grimly. "No further questions." He seated himself at his table.

The black-robed judge leaned on his elbows and clasped his hands. "Mr. Hellinger?"

Hellinger's assistant leaned over to whisper something in his ear. Nick shrugged him off. In front of him on the table, he tinkered with an ornate pocket watch, contemplating the Roman numerals.

"Mr. Hellinger?" the judge repeated, a little more firmly, "do you wish to cross-examine?"

Nick did not look up. His voice was low, but solid, and carried well. "Mr. Lasky, when the defendant boarded the bus, were you headed east or west on Market Street?"

"East." The bus driver nodded. "It was east."

"In other words"—now Nick looked up, his heavy-lidded eyes looking sleepy—"you were headed *toward* the scene of the murder instead of away from it." He raised his eyebrows. "Now *that's* an interesting direction for a man to be escaping in, wouldn't you agree, Mr. Lasky?"

"Objection!" The prosecutor was on his feet.

"Never mind," Nick said laconically. "No further questions."

The prosecutor flashed Nick a hard look. "The people rest, Your Honor."

The judge looked back and forth between prosecutor and defense attorney. "Does the defense wish to call any witnesses at this time?"

Nick sighed. He stole a look at the prosecutor. The sharp young guy who had been prosecuting the case, Alan Handler, was sick, and had been replaced by this guy, even younger, more easily provoked, less careful. Too bad. Nick rose slowly behind the table, looked down at the old pocket watch, then nodded to the judge. "Just one, Your Honor. We call Eloise McIntyre."

The prosecutor bounced again to his feet. "Your Honor, this is ridiculous! Defense is calling the state's key witness—an *eyewitness*, in fact, to the stabbing of Esther Lewis. When she testified, he didn't—"

"Mr. Pollitz," Nick broke in with his deep voice, "why don't you conduct your case? Let me conduct mine."

"But, but," Pollitz sputtered, "Your Honor, Miss McIntyre has already identified the defendant—"

"I thought I heard you say, 'The People rest,'" Nick said, smiling. "That was a short nap."

"Gentlemen, please." The judge lowered his heavy brows authoritatively. "Mr. Pollitz, suppose we let the defense call any witness it chooses. Call Eloise McIntyre."

Nick signaled to his assistant, who quickly left the table and went back through the courtroom to the double doors. He pulled one open, and a woman entered, glanced nervously around, then strode to the witness stand.

She was heavy-set, in her late twenties, with a bouffant hairdo tinged red, wearing a neatly tailored leisure suit that fit her a bit too snugly, and pink-tinted glasses.

The clerk stepped in front of her. "Please state your name for the record."

"Eloise McIntyre," she said softly.

The judge leaned toward her. "Remember you are still sworn, Miss McIntyre. Proceed, Mr. Hellinger."

"Let's swear her again," Nick said, "if you don't mind. Just for the record."

"Mr. Hellinger, I'm sure there's no need for—"

"I'd feel better, okay?" Nick smiled humbly.

"As you wish."

Miss McIntyre was sworn to tell the truth, the whole truth, and nothing but the truth, so help her, God.

"Now, Mr. Hellinger?"

"Thank you, Your Honor." Nick came around the table to stand near her. "Miss McIntyre, on the evening of April third at approximately ten-fifty p.m., did you see the defendant stab and kill the victim, Esther Lewis?"

"No, I did not."

"No further questions," Nick said quickly before anybody could react.

The prosecutor jumped to his feet, members of the jury looked at each other, the judge eyed the witness.

"Now wait a minute," the prosecutor said, coming to the front. "Miss McIntyre, yesterday morning in this courtroom, did you or did you not positively identify the defendant as the man who killed your friend?"

"No, I did not," the woman said smoothly, her chin high.

"Miss McIntyre," the prosecutor glared, "I don't know what you think you're doing, but let me warn you—strike that." Nick was smiling at him. He scratched his forehead, then looked pleadingly at the judge. "Your Honor, I don't know what's going on around here." He stared at the woman, then suddenly took a step back. "This isn't my witness! This isn't Eloise McIntyre!"

Nick strolled over to his side. "She may not be your witness, counselor, but she certainly is Eloise McIntyre. Or couldn't you tell the difference—at a distance of only fifteen feet?" He gestured to scan the space from the witness chair to the prosecutor's table.

Pollitz clenched his hands and jutted out his jaw. "This is another one of your cheap tricks!"

The befuddled judge banged the gavel. "Gentlemen, gentlemen! Order! I will have order here!" He gazed at both of them under furrowed brows. "Now, Mr. Hellinger, what *is* going on here?"

"Your Honor, we have contended from the outset that Miss McIntyre—that is, the state's witness—was too far away from the actual incident to identify positively my client or anybody else. It was raining, it was dark—"

"This is an imposter!" Pollitz shouted.

"I never claimed she was your witness, counselor."

"She gave her name as Eloise McIntyre!"

"Which it is." Nodding, Nick ambled back to the defense table and picked up some papers which he ruffled through. "She had it legally changed, unh, recently in the state of New Jersey. It isn't my fault, counselor, that you—and with all due respect, the Bench"—he glanced up at the judge—"assumed it was the same woman you saw yesterday morning in the witness chair. Just as it is not my client's fault"—his voice took on more power and he fixed the prosecutor with a steely gaze—"that your witness *assumed* she saw my client commit an act of murder—a mistaken identity under far more difficult circumstances!"

"Just a minute!"

"Just the law, counselor!"

"Gentlemen! Order!" The judge whacked his gavel down. "I'll see both of you in my chambers!"

• • •

When he emerged from the court, Nick was not surprised to find a gaggle of media people waiting for him—it was a sensational trial, after all. Strobes flashed in his eyes, microphones were thrust at his mouth. The big eye of a TV minicam was aimed at him from a cameraman's shoulder. He touched his hat in salute to the press.

As he came down the steps, the sea of newspeople parted deferentially, but reluctantly, before the famous and familiar attorney, their voices spilled over each other.

"Mr. Hellinger, can you tell us what went on in the judge's chambers?"

"Did the judge make any ruling about the case?"

"How did you find the mystery woman, Mr. Hellinger?"

"Do you think you'll be brought up before the Bar Association?"

"Prosecutor Pollitz, sir, he mentioned it was a possibility."

"Oh, really?" Nick smiled and moved on down the steps.

"What about your phony witness?" The questioner was a TV woman of whom Nick was fond. "The DA called it another one of your cheap tricks."

"Hey, Sally"—he reached beyond the microphone to touch her arm, and gave her a warm smile—"she was no phony witness. She was duly sworn. A surprise, maybe, but not phony." He waggled a finger at her as if admonishing a child, but never dropped the smile. "You're too smart to use a word like 'phony.'"

She blushed. Reporters liked him, and they basked in any personal attention he gave them.

"What about the 'cheap-trick' aspect?" Sally persisted, again holding out her mike. "Those are the DA's words, not mine." Other mikes joined hers.

Nick stopped at the bottom step and they pressed in around him. "Hey, look, everybody. My client's innocent. My client's life is not cheap. And then, there's Hellinger's Law, right Sally? This one is: When you're on the side of justice, today's cheap trick becomes tomorrow's precedent. I gotta get going."

He moved off through them.

"When's the trial going to resume?" someone called.

"Wednesday, ten a.m."

"We heard something about the real McIntyre woman being recalled—"

"There are two real McIntyre women." Nick smiled slyly.

"—and put under hypnosis to confirm her identification."

"No comment."

"Mr. Hellinger, can you—"

"Okay, everybody." He turned to face them and spread his arms, "I'm running late and I gotta keep my trap shut about specifics right now, okay? See you all Wednesday morning. Have a nice weekend."

They obeyed, letting him go. He walked quickly around the corner of the courthouse, then stopped short at what he saw. "Hey!"

A Traffic Division towtruck had his Mercedes hoisted up and ready for towing.

"Hey, Pete!" Nick ran over to the towtruck driver, who looked shyly away. "Pete, give me a break. This is the third time this month."

"Sorry, Mr. Hellinger." Pete sounded truly sorry. "I keep telling you, it's a red zone."

"And where am I supposed to park, Independence Hall? Who called you, the DA's office? Come on, put her down."

"Please, Mr. Hellinger, you know I can't do that. I already filled out the sheet."

"Yeah, yeah." Nick watched with resignation as his beautiful black sportscar was hauled away. At least Pete was careful with it.

He flagged down a cab, slid into the back, and leaned forward to the driver. "You know Simmy's Place on Chestnut?"

"Do I? Best hoagies in the state."

"Let's go."

There were a hundred small ways Nick held onto his roots. It was a kind of secret strength he had, kept him from being awed or intimidated by anybody or anything. From his days as a kid growing up in a dark, cramped tenement on New York's Lower East Side, the son of a diligent Greek delicatessen owner, he had asserted himself in street scraps and enjoyed heavy sandwiches afterward. He had pride in thinking he hadn't changed all that much. Street scraps were now replaced by more decorous confrontations in the courtroom. But even now, at forty-four and one of the most prominent criminal attorneys around, Nick still emitted the aura of being willing and able to beat you any way it took. And he still craved heavy sandwiches.

He went in under the sign that read: Simmy's Place—Home of the Original All-American Hoagie. He got his sandwiches in a brown paper bag and returned to the cab.

"You hungry?" he asked the driver.

"Pardon?"

"Here." Nick reached over the seat with a hoagie. "Enjoy."

"Really? Wow, thanks a lot. Yeah, I'm starved. How much do I owe—"

"Let's roll. I gotta get back to my office."

"Yes, sir. I know where it is, Mr. Hellinger."

Where it was was not necessarily where Nick would have preferred it to be. His heritage was not upper-class Colonial, and he found no particular pride in having an office in a Society Hill townhouse, one of those wonderful restorations dating back to the days of Ben Franklin. He might have felt more at home in an honest, ordinary office building. But neither was he fussy either way. This is where the judge had long had his office, and Nick loved the judge. Nick would have taken an office anywhere to be in partnership with the grand old man from whom he had learned so much. Oh, yes, the judge came from from a different level of society, but underneath that dignified crust there beat a heart much like Nick's own. Judge Carroll was a fighter.

A small white sign beside the doorway carried the year the place was built, 1782. Beneath that was a white wooden scroll on which was painted in black script: CARROLL & HELLINGER, Attorneys at Law.

The reception room, once a parlor, was small and neat, with hanging plants in the windows, a couple of chairs and a small sofa, all of well-worn leather, and an ample wooden desk. Behind the desk was a small hallway, and off that to either side were the partners' offices.

Dottie was not at her desk, which was not unusual. Carrying his attaché case in one hand and his bag of hoagies in the other, Nick paused at the desk to scan it for notes, saw nothing for him, and started into the hall.

"Did you have an appointment?" came a small voice.

Nick turned back, saw nothing, raised an eyebrow. He stepped beside the reception desk, pursed his lips, then stooped to look.

His eyes met the small, bright, bespectacled eyes of Julie Braden, on her hands and knees under the desk. She blinked.

"It's okay," Nick said reassuringly, "I work here."

"I'm Julie." She lowered her head and felt around the carpet with her hands.

"I'm Nick. Pardon me for asking a dumb question, but why are you under there?"

"I'm looking for my lucky shamrock." She had a lisp.

"Ah. Well, who knows what might be growing under there."

"Not growing. It's a charm."

"Then it's important." He put his sandwich bag and his hat on the desk and the attaché case on the floor, then got down on his own hands and knees to help her look.

"I don't really lisp," she said matter-of-factly. "It's these braces." She bared her wired teeth to him. "Mom says we're making the orthodontist rich."

"Every little bit helps."

"Glasses are a drag too, but Mom says I can't have contacts until I'm older."

"On you, they're beautiful. I like braces too."

"What happened to your hair?"

Nick clapped a hand to the top of his head with mock alarm. "Is it gone again? Merciful heavens! The minute you take your eyes off it, it runs off to play with the raccoons."

Julie giggled. "You shouldn't feel bad about it. Baldness is a sign of virility."

"That a fact?"

"I read it."

"Let's hope it's true. How old are you, Julie?"

"Fourteen."

"Really?"

"Well, twelve."

"Let's settle on ten."

"How did you know?"

"I'm so virile." His fingers closed over a small, round object. "*Voilà*"—he held it up, the leaves embedded in lucite the size of a silver dollar—"your vagrant talisman."

"My shamrock! Oh, wow, thanks!"

Dottie's voice from above: "Contributing to the delinquency of a minor?"

Nick started to rise, bumping his head. He slowly backed out from under the desk and stood up.

Dottie Singer was in the open door to the hall, a watering can in one hand. Black, pretty, lean as a model, in her late thirties, a widow with two children, she was the most efficient and trustworthy woman around, in Nick's opinion. She managed everything in the office that didn't require legal training.

"You have the mind of a vice cop, Singer," Nick said, rubbing his head.

"I've always had an interest in it."

"Why I love you. Do me a favor, make arrangements to get my car bailed out, hunh?"

"Again?"

"Don't get wise, sweetheart, you're dealing with a hungry man."

"Don't I know." She went over to the window to water the plants.

Julie sat in one of the visitors' chairs beside which was a Neiman-Marcus department-store bag. She took needles and yarn from the bag and began knitting studiously.

Dottie motioned toward the hallway. "Judge wants to see you. He says you should come right in without an appointment, don't stand on ceremony, because his days are numbered."

"Cute." He went over to her and said under his breath, "Never mind him, what's with Little Miss Marker there? You running a day-care center on the side?"

"Her mother's waiting in your office. She figured it was better if she met with you alone."

Julie suddenly stopped her knitting, and looked up, wide-eyed. "*You're* Mr. Hellinger?"

"Yeah, why not? Somebody's got to be."

"Then this is for you." She lay aside her knitting, slid off her chair, and came over.

"What?"

"This." She held out the lucky shamrock in the palm of her hand.

"For me?"

"Yes." She nodded vigorously. "On account of my dad. I know you're very good. But you've also got to be lucky, Mr. Hellinger. You've just gotta!"

He let her put the shamrock into his hand as he gazed into her entreating face. "Okay, sunshine. I think you mean it."

"I do! Now you'll be lucky."

"Hmm." He looked at Dottie. "Tell this young lady's mother that I'll only be a moment."

"She's very, um . . ."

26

"Yeah, well, tell her to relax. I'm gonna be lucky, whatever it is."

He picked up the bag of hoagies from the desk and headed in for Judge Carroll's office.

Howard Taft Carroll, a distinguished, white-haired man nearing seventy who was born on the day of Taft's inauguration as President, sat behind his big oak desk. His dark suit was neatly pressed, his dark tie neatly in place. He held his pen properly as learned in grammar school. He was the picture of a prim and precise professional man. He was called "Judge" by nearly everyone because he was for years a justice of the Pennsylvania Supreme Court. He had become an active Democrat—dismaying his parents—and served two terms in Congress during the Truman administration. Over the years he had not lost any of his combative edge or legal brilliance.

Nick knocked lightly at the door, and Judge Carroll looked up from the brief he had been perusing.

"Ah, Nicholas, come in, come in."

Nick put the bag of hoagies on the judge's desk before sitting. "I ordered you two."

"Not hoagies."

"What do you think, shish kabob?"

"It'll ruin my stomach."

Nick shrugged and reached for the bag. The judge batted his hand away. "Now, Nick, surely I was misinformed about what occurred in court today?"

"Depends, Judge. A lot went on."

"I heard about your so-called witness . . ."

"I was feeling playful. But did you also hear, for example, that the prosecution may have to reexamine its key witness under hypnosis?"

"Hypnosis?" The judge leaned back in his tall swivel chair and made a steeple of his hands. He gave a hint of a smile. "I don't suppose that was your idea."

"Well, I try to assist in the course of justice however I can. I might have mentioned it to Judge Poret in chambers."

"And they bought it, Judge Poret and young Handler both?"

"Pollitz is handling the case now, Handler is sick. Anyway, we'll know Wednesday. Anything to get at the truth."

"How did you talk them into it?"

"Charm. Soon as Pollitz decided it was his own idea, he bit. The lady was mistaken in her identification, Judge. It'll come out, under hypnosis."

"You also planning to charm the Bar Association?"

"My, my, you heard a lot, didn't you?"

"I'm afraid the district attorney's office was quite upset."

"If Pollitz is *that* upset, I may need a good lawyer. How's your schedule?"

"Busy. Well, Nicholas, you're being a little devilish in this case, are you not?"

"My client's innocent."

"Even so... but I think I'll withhold the usual lecture until I see if your little flim-flam succeeds."

"You're getting soft, Judge."

"Don't count on it."

"Mellow, then."

"One does mellow. Ah, yes. By the way, I'll be spending the weekend in Atlantic City with a young lady."

"Young lady?"

"Bert Raskin's widow."

"Oh, *that* young lady. She'll appreciate the description."

"To me, sixty-two is young."

28

"Why not? Age is in the mind."

"And you?"

"Work."

"Come now, Nicholas, you always find time for—"

"Maybe I'll get lucky, then. I got a shamrock." He held it up.

"You're not still seeing that last one I met—what's her name? Susan?"

"Susan wants a house and garden."

"You have to settle down sometime."

"Not this weekend, Judge."

"Ah, me. Well, run along now, Nick." He gave a cursory wave of the hand. "Doesn't do to keep a prospective client waiting too long. They tend to get churlish."

"I don't need another client, churlish or otherwise."

"I know. It's a big case, Nick."

"You've talked to her."

"Dottie tried to put her off, get her to make an appointment. She wouldn't leave. Make her feel better, at least. Recommend somebody. Peter Felcher would be good, from Austin. More familiar with Texas law. Calm her down. You're good at that."

"Thanks." Nick reached for the sandwich bag.

"You can leave that."

Nick grinned and headed for his own office across the hall.

When he opened the door, her eyes were fixed on it as if she had been staring at it forever. Nice blue eyes, blond hair pulled back in a bun, pleasant face except for the tension in it; trim figure in a nice blue suit. Nice legs. She sat primly erect, one nice leg in front of the other.

"Mr. Hellinger!"

"Hello." He closed the door behind him and went across to shake hands with her. She was very tight. "And you are?"

"Cara Braden."

"I met your daughter, Julie, outside. Delightful." He went behind his desk to sit down, then saw that several newspapers had been put spread on his desk for him to see, issues of the *Houston Herald*. He paused, leaning on his hands, and looked over at her.

"It's all there, Mr. Hellinger. I mean, the awful publicity. On the front pages. About my husband. None of it's true. I mean, there was a murder, but Lon didn't do it. I mean, it's not possible. It just isn't—"

He held up a hand to stop her and, still standing, scanned the headlines: "NEWSCASTER SLAIN!"; "PAUL SAVAGE MURDERED IN HOME"; "LOCAL TV PERSONALITY BRUTALLY MURDERED: ACCOUNTANT HELD."

"Lon didn't do it, Mr. Hellinger! I can explain—"

"Please, Mrs. Braden, just give me a minute, okay?" He smiled consolingly at her. "Let me get the gist of it here first."

"Sorry." She folded her hands nervously in her lap and stared down at them.

The stories described who Paul Savage was, how he was found dead, apparently brained by a poker; how because of his exposés he had many enemies; how the police had arrested Alonzo Braden at the scene—Braden a CPA whose major client was the diversified conglomerate Trans-Texas Industries; how Braden proclaimed his innocence. Circumstantial evidence was heavy. Pictures showed Braden, a nice-looking man, ordinary build, perhaps late thirties; handcuffed, his business suit disheveled, his hair mussed and wet, trouser legs muddy. Two uniformed policemen were guiding him by the elbows.

Nick nodded. "Not pleasant," he said softly.

"Awful! Lies!" She cleared her throat, trying to control herself. "Accused of killing a journalist, that's why all the stories!"

"Well, it seems that the deceased was quite a prominent—"

"Journalist! Never mind Paul Savage was the lowest form of animal life, the fraternity closes ranks!"

"Mrs. Braden, with all due respect, let me suggest that the main matter here is not the journalism fraternity. This kind of thing, there would be big stories, any prominent person who—"

"Against the Houston press corps, a local lawyer hasn't a prayer!"

"I see." Nick seated himself behind the desk and eyed the newspapers. Cara Braden sniffled lightly, and took out a lace handkerchief to dab her nose. It was natural for her to be distraught, common for him to feel sympathetic. But there were so many clients and potential clients begging for help, so many people craving his sympathy and legal protection.

"Mrs. Braden," he said evenly, "I'm very sorry about what has happened. Your husband obviously needs an attorney, and from the looks of this, he needs a heavyweight. But my calendar is jammed right now. I don't mean to seem cold about it, and I'm not. But I've got a case in court—a murder case, in fact—that resumes on Wednesday. Two more serious and demanding ones pending after that, and several others waiting for attention. Each one is serious, with lives at stake, so I am extremely tied up, and—"

"I wouldn't be here if you were advertising for clients!"

"No." He studied her. She was trying so hard to maintain composure. This was quite clearly an uncharacteristic job for her, to try to represent her husband in a crucial matter. She seemed like a housewife suddenly cast in a terrible new role. But she was tough. Nick admired that. "I'd like to suggest a lawyer to you, an excellent man, in Austin, in whom I feel quite confident—"

"You, Mr. Hellinger. That's who I want. Nobody from Texas. You. Lon needs you. You're the one man in this country I would feel confident in."

"I'm flattered, Mrs. Braden. I wish I could help you. That's the truth. But the fact is, there are other lawyers who may not have the public reputation, but are every bit as able. This lawyer I want to recommend to you is—"

"You! Please understand me, Mr. Hellinger. I'm not ignorant about this. I know about other lawyers. That's why I came all this way. You can save my husband. He's innocent."

"It's regrettable that you made such a long trip. Perhaps if you had phoned first, I could have recommended—"

"Yes, it's so much easier to say no over the telephone."

"I wasn't thinking about making it easier for myself, but for you."

"If it's the money..."

"Believe me, it's not the money."

"Lon's biggest account is Trans-Texas Industries. You know of that company, of course."

"Certainly."

"They flew me here in a private jet. That's how much they think of Lon! And you!"

"Mrs. Braden, I'm sure your husband is worthy of all possible support."

"My husband is a lot more than that!"

Tenacious as a bulldog. He wasn't doing very well. "Please don't misunderstand me, I didn't mean to suggest that your husband is not worthy of me; quite the opposite, really. I'm afraid that I couldn't give him the attention he deserves, given my—"

"Listen to me!" She was on the edge of her chair. Her words tumbled out. "I married Alonzo Braden when I was seventeen, Mr. Hellinger. He's the only man I've ever . . . known." She bowed her head demurely for a moment, then looked up and resumed pell-mell. "Up until two days ago, I was the world's most dependent woman, and happy with it. Lon took care of Julie and me, took care of everything. We did everything together. He gave me a perfect life. Then suddenly he wasn't there."

There was a hitch in her voice, and she paused for a moment to gather herself. Nick refrained from saying anything, though he would have liked to say she was unfairly denigrating herself.

"It was like waking up a widow." She hesitated. "Don't you see? This is the first chance I've had to give something back! Don't make me fail, Mr. Hellinger. Don't . . ."

Tears welled up and rolled down her cheeks. She shook her head, unable to continue. She sagged in the chair, wringing the delicate handkerchief in her hands, occasionally patting her eyes. She coughed, blew her nose, lay her head back against the chair and blinked, gazing at the ceiling.

Nick idly tossed the lucky shamrock in his hand. "You don't play fair, Mrs. Braden," he said softly, smiling crookedly.

"I'm sorry, I—"

"I walked out of that courtroom this afternoon feeling pretty good about myself—doing a good job for an innocent client, being a little daring, using good imagination—feeling like I was a pretty good lawyer and a pretty good guy. Now I'll go home looking for a dog to kick."

Sniffling, her voice shaky, she said, "If you could just come to Houston, meet Lon, then you would know. You would know how important it is, how right it is." She looked up at him, a flicker of hope still in her wet eyes. "You said yourself you don't have to be in court until Wednesday."

"Yeah." This lady, for all her distress, didn't miss a thing.

"Damn, damn, damn! I swore to myself I wouldn't cry."

"Don't be so hard on yourself. I would have advised you not to swear. Nothing wrong with crying." People cried in Nick's office all the time—they came there, after all, with serious problems. But he felt helpless to ease her distress.

There was a soft knock at the door, it opened, Dottie came in carrying an elegant silver coffee tray with steaming china cups. She quickly took in the scene, glanced at Nick, put the tray down on the coffee table, and said quietly to Cara, "We also stock the stronger stuff—maybe some brandy?"

Cara abruptly got to her feet, shaking her head. "No, thank you. Thanks for everything. I was just leaving."

Nick had turned away and was looking out the door down the hall to the reception room. In his angle of vision, he could see little Julie calmly knitting in the chair. It wasn't fair; he was such a softy. But also it struck him as a curious kind of tough case, and he was a sucker for that too.

He swiveled back. "Sit down, Mrs. Braden, please?"

34

She blinked quizzically.

"Please." He held his hand out, gesturing to her chair. Dottie discreetly backed out and shut the door.

Cara sat slowly down. Nick fingered the shamrock in front of him, where she could see it. "Can you wait a minute while I make a couple of quick phone calls?"

"Beg your pardon?"

"Unh"—he rubbed his chin and smiled—"you said something about Houston. May I join you? You can fill me in on the plane."

She did fill him in, as much as she could, given her moods that shifted between gratitude and hope because Nick was with her, and fears about her husband. From what she told him, they did in fact have a good life together, with enormous affection between them. But there was a lot about her husband's work she didn't seem to know.

She said that Lon didn't talk much about his work—he was an accountant, after all, what was there to tell? And she didn't care all that much for Trans-Texas Industries. She wasn't particularly fond of the people Lon dealt with there—she didn't know why, exactly, just not her type of people, she guessed. Not Lon's either. And she resented the demands of time and concentration the company made on her husband.

She and Lon were both from Chicago, had been married there, and then moved to Houston several years ago for this job. The city, she said, had a lot to offer and an interesting mix of people from all over who worked in science (particularly the space program) and in the arts and medicine and oil. But the Bradens weren't crazy about the place, even so.

"Mainly," she said, "I think it's the weather. Everything's air-conditioned, but we were really used to Chicago, you know, and the lake, and vacations in the north woods. Seasons."

"I know what you mean, about seasons. This job must have been very attractive, to cause you to move."

"*Very.* Lon is really a top-flight accountant, and they provide very well. All kinds of benefits and so on. They trust Lon with a lot of stuff. Some of the stuff he doesn't talk about because, he says, it is really top-secret private business stuff. You know how much industrial spying goes on?"

"I know something about it."

"It's incredible! So Lon has to keep a lot of things to himself—not because he doesn't trust me, you understand, but because he maintains a habit of keeping his mouth shut, so he won't make any slips. And all the tax stuff, you know, how businesses put their money here and there to avoid high taxes. I'm not crazy about that aspect of it. Lon isn't either. But that's the way it is."

"That's the way it is."

They sat in a double seat in the small, fast Lear Jet. Julie sat behind them, knitting like a pro. Now and then Cara turned back to her to ask how she was. She was always fine.

Once Julie stood to lean over their seat between them. "Mr. Hellinger, will you get Daddy out of jail?"

He put a hand on her blond ponytail. "Bet on it, honey."

"I'm glad." She put a hand on his head. "So smooth."

"It's plastic. My real head starts down here." He stroked his prominent nose.

She laughed. "You're silly."

"Yeah."

"But you're a very good lawyer, aren't you? Mommy said."

"Yeah, sunshine."

When Julie had sat back down, Cara said softly, "I can't tell you how grateful I am."

"Don't bother. It's better than chasing ambulances."

"You're always teasing."

"Not always. I can be a very serious shyster, under the right circumstances."

"You're not. A shyster, I mean. You have a fantastic reputation, you know."

"Don't bother about that either. Cases don't make a lawyer's reputation."

"I know. Sometimes I feel so scared about it. About Lon, I mean, what might happen." She turned to look closely into his eyes. "You *are* the right choice for this, aren't you? I mean, they were right having me come after you?"

"Yeah. Probably."

CHAPTER 3

THEY LANDED at night—the Houston skyline lit up several miles beyond the airport—and they were met at the plane by a liveried driver.

"Welcome back, Mrs. Braden," he said, touching his black cap.

"Thank you, Leo. Nick, this is Leo. Leo, Attorney Hellinger."

The driver escorted them through the terminal, trailed by a skycap wheeling a cart with their luggage.

A Cadillac limousine was waiting at curbside. Leo ushered Nick, Cara, and Julie into the back seat, then left them to assist the skycap in loading the luggage into the trunk.

Nick pursed his lips. "Private plane. Private limo. I'll expect a basket of fruit in my hotel room."

Cara blushed.

"Relax, Mrs. Braden, I know when I'm being courted, and by whom. None of this matters. I'm interested in your husband, not his company."

"Thank you." She did relax a little.

Nick climbed the steps into the County Jail reception area and approached the desk. The officer on duty behind it was reading a magazine. To his side at a cabinet, his back to Nick, a plainclothesman in shirtsleeves wearing a shoulder holster was examining a file.

Nick cleared his throat, the duty officer looked up. "My name is Hellinger. I'm a lawyer here to see Braden."

"Oh, yes, sir. Detective Sergeant Donovan has been expecting you." He turned to the plainclothesman. "Sergeant Donovan?"

Donovan glanced back. "Yeah?"

"Mr. Hellinger."

"Oh, yeah." Donovan smiled at Nick, seeming almost to wink at the same time. He picked his jacket off a chairback and shrugged himself into it as he came over. He stuck out his large hand. "Mr. Hellinger, Roy Donovan. Welcome to Houston."

"The pleasure's all mine." Nick didn't smile as they shook hands. "You're the detective in charge of the investigation?"

"I'm it." He steered Nick into the hall leading to the holding cells. "Not a tough one, though, from my point of view. Pretty much open and shut. Guess you probably already heard or read enough to know the prisoner's got nothing going for him, guilty as hell."

"Naturally. What sane lawyer would travel this far to defend an innocent man? Young local boy could do that."

"I'm not saying he shouldn't be *represented*, of course."

"The American way. You got coffee in the lawyer's room?"

"I'll have some sent in, if you want."

"Yeah, a pot. Jet lag, biologic clock, it's late for me."

It was a grim, nearly bare room, green paint flecking off the walls, a rectangular table in the center on which was an ashtray, and three wooden chairs. The room's single, high window was barred on the outside. Nick took a yellow legal pad from his case, put it on the table, leaned back, and waited.

Shortly Braden was brought in. They nodded greetings to each other, then Braden lit a cigarette and began to pace.

He was unshaven and haggard, and dressed in faded, baggy jailhouse denims, but Nick would have recognized him anyway from the newspaper pictures. His brown hair was neatly cut and combed. His features were pleasant and regular, nothing remarkable perhaps to the ordinary observer. He was nervous, and avoided eye contact with Nick. And it was the eyes, Nick felt, that suggested something beyond the ordinary. Braden's eyes were especially intense and alert.

Nick watched him pace for a few minutes, then tapped his ballpoint on the yellow pad.

Braden stopped and looked at him. "How are they, Mr. Hellinger?"

"They seem fine. Worried, of course, but otherwise okay. How are you?"

"Fine." He chuckled humorlessly and resumed pacing.

"So much for the social amenities, Mr. Braden. We'd better get down to business."

"Business," Braden mumbled.

"Let's talk about murder."

Braden stopped, facing the wall, as if the word had stung and immobilized him. "Murder," he repeated.

"Yeah."

"Did I do it? No."

Nick waited, Braden didn't offer more. "Not much of an explanation, Mr. Braden. You were there, et cetera, et cetera. Come on."

"Yes, yes, for chrissake, I was there. I found the body. I was arrested." He mumbled something else Nick couldn't hear.

"I like it when a client looks me in the eye, Mr. Braden. Especially when he's only a *prospective* client."

"Prospective?"

"Like there's an echo in here. Yes, prospective." He didn't give much away, Nick thought, plays it very coy. "We don't have a lot of time, my friend, so it doesn't help to use it playing games. Everybody's a prospective client until I hear their story. Until I'm sure they're being honest with me."

"You don't think I'm innocent."

"Innocent, guilty, that's not the point. The point is you're not telling me anything. I'm not a dentist. You've got to do more than just open and say 'Ah' and wait for me to look around in your mouth."

Braden chuckled again, again without mirth, but with recognition of the analogy, at least. He was paying attention.

"You want to know what I was doing there."

"It's a thought. Suppose I believed you were innocent—just to pick a position at random. It would help to know what you were doing there, considering that less than an hour earlier you'd been heard to make a threat against the victim's life."

"A threat?"

"That girl at the studio. You mentioned strangulation."

"That. Jesus. Yeah, it was in the papers. What a—"

He stopped when there was a knock at the door. It opened, Donovan stood in it.

"Mr. Hellinger?"

"Just put in on the table." Nick didn't turn, kept his eyes on Braden.

"I didn't bring the coffee, because District Attorney Whedon wants to see you in his office."

"Not now."

"I'm sorry, Mr. Hellinger, but—"

"*Later*, dammit! I'm talking to my client!"

Donovan's voice was flat. "He says it might have a bearing on what you want to talk to your client about."

Braden flinched. Nick now turned sharply to Donovan. The detective stood impassively, stoop-shouldered, a hint of a sneer on his face.

"What the hell is this?" Nick growled.

"Just giving you the message."

Nick thought for a moment, then motioned him out. "In a minute."

"I'll be right down the hall." Donovan backed out. "I'll take you over there."

Nick waited several seconds after the door was closed, then turned slowly back toward Braden. "All right, you want to tell me what this is likely to be about, or you want me to be surprised?"

"I really don't know what it's about."

"Yeah, right. Well, maybe he'll save you the trouble of telling me the story." He tossed the legal pad back into his briefcase, slammed the case shut, and stalked out of the room.

Nick did not like it. It wasn't just that he was being interrupted in his first visitation with his client. It wasn't just that Braden seemed to be holding back. Sometimes you got a straight story from a client right away, sometimes not. You couldn't make too much out of that. But every case had a feel to it. There were nuances, suggestions, things in the wind that a sensitive defense attorney picked up. Nick was keenly attuned to attitudes that surrounded a case. It was complicated, no more than hints and hunches—not just about guilt or innocence, but about methods, styles, egos, confidences. How he sensed these things helped him determine his approach to the case.

He did not like the feel of this case. There were too many things in the air he couldn't get a fix on. They knew who he was down here—those on both sides of the case. And they knew he wasn't just another high-priced criminal lawyer. It was unlikely that they were taking him lightly. His reputation was certainly not that of a lawyer who could be pushed around or toyed with. He certainly wasn't hungry for clients. If he was partial to the plight of little kids whose daddys were in trouble, well, it was just because kids were truly innocent. And because they didn't deserve to have daddys in trouble.

But he couldn't believe anybody was devilish enough to have sent little Julie Braden along with her mother just because he could be taken in by the child.

And although her presence at his office had triggered a crucial bit of sympathy for the case, she wasn't the reason he was here. He was here because there was something in the stories about the murder that tugged at him, something curious, mysterious. It didn't quite make sense. He was challenged.

But he wasn't totally committed, not yet, not until he knew what he was getting involved in. And already he had the vague feeling that he was treading on thin ice.

He wasn't in the mood to waste any more time.

He and Donovan did not converse during the walk over to the DA's office. Nick was ushered in ahead of Donovan.

District Attorney Fred Whedon was on the phone. He was in shirtsleeves, leaning far back in his chair, his stockinged feet up on his desk, his eyes on a notepad propped on his thighs.

Across the room, a strikingly attractive, slender woman with long, dark hair was dumping a pouch of coffee into the electric machine. She didn't acknowledge their entrance.

Neither did Whedon. Scowling at his notes, he barked into the phone, "Simple assault? With two eyewitnesses? Irvin must think I'm Santa Claus. What? Hey, we're not *that* busy here. We have time to try cases. Well, you better believe we'll push. Tell that character that maybe we'll settle for aggravated assault. *Maybe*. By Friday." He put down the phone without saying good-bye.

Donovan rapped lightly on the doorframe to attract his attention. "Mr. Whedon? Mr. Hellinger. I'll wait in the hall."

Whedon put his feet down, smiled broadly, and

leaned across the desk, stretching his hand out to Nick. "Welcome to Houston, Mr. Hellinger."

"I've already been welcomed." Nick ignored the hand.

"We try to be friendly."

"Yeah, well, never mind the soap. I'm not in the market for a used car, and it's past my bedtime. You interrupted my train of thought, Whedon. That's not nice. Where I come from, an attorney's visitation privileges with a client are sacred."

"Sit down, sit down." Whedon waved toward a chair. "This won't take long."

"Then I can take it standing."

"Coffee, Mr. Hellinger?" the woman said, smiling. "I'm pouring fresh."

Nick didn't look at her. "No thanks, sugar, and don't try to change the subject. Listen, Whedon, I'm sitting with my client and along comes Dick Tracy there and says the DA wants to see me. So here I am. So far, I am not having a good time. The clock is running. So just tell me how much the bail, how soon he's sprung, and where do I go for a decent taco."

The woman brought a cup of coffee for Whedon and one for herself and sat down, crossing her long legs and balancing her cup on her knee. Plainly no secretary.

"Anne Gronouski," Whedon said, indicating the woman.

"Mr. Hellinger," she acknowledged.

"She'll be handling the prosecution." Whedon kept smiling.

"Like hell she will." Now Nick looked at her, but still directed his words to Whedon. "This case will never go to trial, and you know it."

"Is that a fact?" Anne Gronouski said, arching her

eyebrows and taking a sip of coffee.

Confident lady. Confident and cool and beautiful. If the case ever did go to trial, Nick would have to handle her carefully. She would have everybody's attention to start with, and everybody's sympathy the minute Nick got pushy. Besides, even the way she held her cup suggested she was very much under control. Nick didn't mind seeing sharp young women lawyers on the make for big careers, but they sure as hell could cramp his style. You couldn't run over them. And he didn't want to get into anything with her now. So he ignored her and turned to Whedon, leaning one fist on the desk.

"Let's not play games with each other, Whedon. We are not talking trial here. You sent for me, remember? Which means you want to deal."

"Not necessarily."

"Necessarily!" Nick would have liked to wipe that grin off Whedon's face. Handsome young guy, maybe thirty-five, very curly hair. Nick would have pegged him for a cop, which was only a minor mistake. Now he wanted to push him, see how bright he was. He glanced obviously at his pocket watch. "So you can skip the wherefores and whereases, just give me the bottom line."

Whedon and Anne exchanged glances. Whedon picked up a pencil, twirling it between his palms, and curled his lip into a tighter smile. Goddamned cool act.

"Some information might be interesting to you."

"Not likely, but see if you can get my attention."

"You won't like it."

"I'm already not liking it. I don't like hangovers either, but I've learned to live with them." Nick was tempted to walk out. He half turned from the desk.

"What exactly have you been told about Alonzo Braden?"

"That's not exactly any of your business, counselor."

"I'm not prying."

"Good imitation."

"Well, let me guess. You know he's a self-employed CPA. Good family man. No criminal record. Accused of murdering a man he barely knew. Wife says he's innocent." Whedon cocked his head.

"Very good, Whedon. Too bad I didn't have time to talk to my client, I might have been able to fill you in on a whole lot more."

The sarcasm seemed finally to reach the DA. He stopped smiling and narrowed his eyes. "Did Mrs. Braden by any chance mention Trans-Texas Industries?"

"Oh, yeah, you left that out before. Braden does some work for them. I'll go over his whole resumé first chance I get. I think he mowed lawns as a kid."

Whedon didn't change his expression. "Trans-Texas Industries is owned by a man named Clinton Tolliver. Being an easterner, you probably wouldn't know, of course."

"The name, or what?" He was tempted to reach over and snap that pencil Whedon was manipulating.

Whedon eyed him carefully. "Tolliver's what you might call our local *capo di tutti capo*."

The phrase whacked Nick between the eyes.

"That's right, Mr. Hellinger. For the past several years, Braden's been the chief accountant for organized crime in the state of Texas."

Nick struggled to control himself. "You intend to use that, counselor, you better—you better be ready to—"

"Just thought you should know who you're dealing with, Mr. Hellinger—unless, of course, you're already plugged in."

Nick wasn't going to bite on that last, not here in the DA's office. "Clever idea. Young DA gets a handle on the mob, rises quickly in his profession."

"I have no reason to lie to you, Mr. Hellinger." He smiled at Anne. "Sorry to have spoiled your fun, counselor." He paused. "So it shouldn't be a total loss, I'll be happy to give you the name of a good taco house."

"Forget it. Maybe I'll eat pasta."

Nick defended people he didn't like, even people who were guilty—a premise of the law being that the prosecution must be made to prove its case. But on matters of law he didn't lie. And as one who didn't, he recognized the same trait in others. He didn't think the DA was lying. Whatever else he thought about the cocky young man, Nick was confident that he was telling the truth.

It was enough to take away a man's appetite. If Whedon was trying to scare him off, it was a waste of time. Hellinger's father had been forced to make payoffs to distributors. "For peace," he would say, when Nick was old enough to question. "It's normal, part of the business." But his father worked so hard, for so little, Nick hated that part of the business. When he was a teenager, and street-tough, it was all he could do to stand idly by while his father went into the back room with the squat, scowling man who wore a derby and carried a walking stick.

As a lawyer, one of his early cases—the first during which he received telephone threats, the first that brought him press attention, the first for which he won an acquittal in a murder case—was when he defended a young numbers runner being framed by the mob for killing a banker with a baseball bat and dumping the body in the Delaware River. The guy was a punk kid, a petty crook nobody gave a damn about, nobody wanted to defend, given the circumstances.

But he was not a murderer. Nick took the case, taped the threatening phone calls, and won in court when the prosecutor lied. No, the state did not really have an eyewitness. Or rather, the eyewitness suddenly "couldn't be located." Nick didn't need to introduce the tapes in court. He just stacked them on his defense table. The mob could come after him if it wanted to. But it didn't. The message from the trial was—when you buy a prosecutor and put him up against Nick Hellinger, don't have him lie.

Nick did not like traveling. It gave him heartburn and exacerbated his unforgiving nature.

He banged on the door. Mrs. Braden answered it dressed in a flowered hostess gown. At least she did not have a happy face.

"Let's talk, Mrs. Braden."

"Of course, certainly. You've seen Lon?" She stepped aside to let him enter the living room. "You look upset."

"So do you."

Her eyes were red. So were her hands, as if she had been rubbing them together.

"What's the matter, Mr. Hellinger? Did you talk to Lon?"

"I talked to lots of people, Mrs. Braden. I've been on the road too long already. I don't like the stories I hear when I'm out of town."

"Would you like to sit down?" She pointed toward

the easy chair. It was a nice, large room, a lot of teak and glass. A nice large house, a nice quiet neighborhood. Very peaceful, very good investment. Solid and stable.

"You lied to me, Mrs. Braden." He didn't sit, but put his hat on the chairback.

"What?" She put a hand to her cheek.

"You have a nice place here, Mrs. Braden. Comes with the territory, maybe. I heard a little more about Trans-Texas Industries, and a guy named Clint Tolliver who maybe is a good guy to know, if you're in the market for a nice life." Out of the corner of his eye, he watched her sink into the sofa, now with both her hands on her cheeks. "I don't believe everything I hear. I believe what I heard about your husband's employer or benefactor or cohort—whatever you call him in your private conversations. We aren't exactly talking about private enterprise and industrial spying and tax loopholes, are we, Mrs. Braden? Not quite accurate, how you ran it down for me, hunh? Not quite the truth, Mrs. Braden. I am not a happy man."

"I didn't lie! I just didn't tell you . . . everything."

"Don't split hairs with me, lady. I lost my virginity a hundred years ago on the streets of New York. Once that happens, you never forget it, like riding a bicycle. I lost my virginity on this particular case an hour ago in the DA's office. I don't like being surprised in the DA's office. A good client keeps a lawyer from being surprised in the DA's office."

She clenched her hands around her knees. Her eyes were wet. She leaned forward. "Would you have come to Houston if you had known? Would you? You wouldn't! I didn't dare tell you. I had to get you here to meet Lon, talk to him, see for yourself that he's innocent."

"Well, you did it wrong, baby. I didn't run across any innocence here. Not in your husband, not in you. You used me, both of you. I don't like being used."

"Used you? *Used* you! *Begged* you, Mr. Hellinger, that's what I did. I would have done anything to get you to Houston. At gunpoint, if I had a gun. To save my husband, whatever it took, I would do it."

She got up and faced away from him, folding her arms across her chest. "Sure, I knew who he worked for, what the rumors were, what kind of reputation that man has. I understood a lot. I'm not saying I didn't know. I'm not saying I liked it. I'm not even saying I didn't care. But that never got in the way of how I felt about my husband. What I'm saying is I love Alonzo Braden and that means more to me than how he earns his living. Maybe you wouldn't understand that."

"If I wanted to talk about love, I would've had more effective opportunities in Philadelphia."

She whirled on him. "A snide answer for everything, right? Well, let me tell you some more I don't think you will understand. Lon is honest. I'm not talking about figures in a ledger now. I'm talking about honest the way a wife knows. Nothing in black and white, nothing easy to explain. But underneath the surface, the appearances, underneath the kind of stuff that has made you angry, that makes other people suspicious. Lon has an integrity that defies explanation. I don't even understand it myself, exactly. But I know it's true. And it wouldn't matter what he did, I would trust him, and I could forgive him anything. Anything!"

"Including," Nick said quietly, "murder?"

"Yes, even that!"

"Well, well, well." Nick nodded. "You're a lot of

woman, Mrs. Braden. With you in his corner, maybe a man could feel he could take on the world."

"Nobody's talking about taking on the world."

"Well, we all have our own little worlds to take on, Mrs. Braden. I admire your loyalty. Quite rare. And I guess your husband must have done something to deserve it."

"But . . .?" She anticipated.

"But there are too many warts on this one." Nick shook his head. "When I take on a client, it's because he's been up front with me all the way. Tricks need to be pulled, I'll pull them. But the client doesn't pull them on me. That's just the way I operate. A few times I've been sorry, made the mistake of taking on somebody who wasn't straight with me. But I've never been sorry I took on somebody who was level, even if I had a rotten case. I don't trust you. I don't trust your husband."

"Even after I've told you the truth."

"Oh, yeah, yeah, I think you've leveled some. But only when I confronted you. You held off as long as you could. You'd do it again and not even blink. I'd be walking blindfolded through a minefield. I'd never know for sure whether you were leveling, or holding something back that could pop up in court and get me pinned to the wall. Surprises about your client from the DA, surprises about your client in court—those are like stakes driven through the heart of a defense attorney, Mrs. Braden. No thanks."

He picked up his hat and turned toward the door. Something caught his eye.

Julie Braden, in her pajamas, was perched on the second-floor landing, peering solemnly down at the scene in the living room with her face pressed between the struts of the banister.

He planted his hat on his head and waved to her. He smiled, uncomfortably. "Adios, sunshine."

When he closed the door behind him, he could hear Mrs. Braden break into sobs, and the thump-thump of Julie hurrying down the stairs to her.

Well, it was never pleasant dumping a client, no matter how mean or rotten or dishonest the client was. Because—and it always became apparent just when you said bye-bye—every one of those clients needed, deserved, a lawyer. Not to prove them innocent necessarily, not even to keep them from paying a penalty for a crime. But to keep the prosecution honest, make the state stick to the law. Even guilty people had rights. Otherwise you could just let the cops take them in, let the state put them in jail and forget about them. Nick was no softy about criminals. If he had ever been able to find the guy who robbed and shot his father, he would have dispensed a final, summary justice right on the spot—no lawyers, no arrests. He knew how people felt.

Nor did he have some prissy notion about picking and choosing his clients to suit his fancy just because he was such a big-shot lawyer. The thing was, when Nick took on a client, he put himself on the line for him. Sometimes that was not safe for his career, sometimes it was not safe for his health. But that's why he had to trust the clients to be dealing straight with him.

The fact that he had come so far and spent the time really angered him. And he had been used. He was angry at himself for that; he had let his defenses down, relaxed his vigilance. It amounted to being careless, which he hated and couldn't afford. Also, he was exhausted. And when he was exhausted he tended to get sentimental. He didn't like to hear Mrs. Braden crying, or to see the haunted look in Julie's eyes.

Get married, have a child, settle down, Hellinger—inner voices sometimes whined at him. Especially when he was tired. Everybody got married, had kids, settled down. Nick's mother had left his father when Nick was a baby. Maybe that's why he never could wholly trust the idea. His father had got married, had a kid, settled down, worked his ass off, and been a sad, tired, lonely man when two bullets split his neck and sent him to his reward.

But before that, the old man had made it clear to Nick that he didn't want his son to go the same route. No slaving in a delicatessen. "A profession," he admonished Nick. "Help some people. And not for peanuts, either. A doctor. That's why I work. I put money away for you. Don't worry."

So there was money for school. But Nick didn't want to be a doctor. A doctor couldn't have helped his father, who was dead before he hit the floor. The law could have helped him, earlier. He shouldn't have had to pay "for peace" in his store. Nick wanted to help with the law. He wanted to be a cop. Experiences in Korea redirected him somewhat.

So then home, to Columbia, Harvard, assistant in the U.S. Attorney's office. He developed a taste for putting criminals in jail.

But there was another side to it. There were a lot of little people who were pushed around by dishonest people on both sides of the law. Society needed to be protected against crooks, and little people needed to be protected against the crookedness of society. And they couldn't afford to hire good lawyers. So Nick resigned from the prosecutor's office and set up his own law practice. He was good, he was successful, his practice grew, and he earned a reputation for integrity. Even prosecutors trusted him—they didn't like his courtroom tricks, but they knew he played fair. He used his knowledge and his wiles to keep the prosecutors honest. Korea had taught him the importance of that.

And that was what attracted Howard Taft Carroll to him. Carroll knew the other side too, as a prosecutor and judge. He was established, eminently successful and secure and wealthy. He liked the idea of having a youthful, ambitious, scrupulous partner to keep him honest, to remind him of the ideals of justice, to keep him young.

Lord, Nick was tired. He dropped off his rented car with the doorman of the hotel and went groggily to his room and slept till noon.

The next afternoon, he dawdled. He watched the Texas-Arkansas game on TV, rooting hard for Arkansas just because he was in a very un-Texas mood. He considered taking an evening flight. He felt like having company, somebody to meet him at the airport and make him feel better. He ran up a long-distance bill. He called Joanne, no answer. He called Jillian, she was otherwise engaged. Kate, Diana, Andrea—the lot of them, all out or busy or something. He even tried Susan, but hung up when she answered. Her feelings were too serious, and he had scruples about that.

He didn't feel like going home alone, not tonight. So he would fly back tomorrow.

He dozed, he watched TV, he summoned food and drink up from room service. He had a relaxing day, what he needed.

He had finished supper, dozed off again, when the phone rang. It was Judge Carroll.

"Well, Judge, a friendly voice. I assume you're

at leisure, at least. Well, so am I. What's up?"

"Not much, Nicholas. I'm just here at the office, looking over a mess of very long briefs spread out on the desk, enjoying the delicacy of egg salad on rye."

"The office? I thought you were in Atlantic City. What happened?"

"It's pouring rain."

"Who cares what it does outside at night? It's not raining on the craps tables."

"The lady doesn't shoot craps and I don't play bingo, and we're both coming down with colds. Ah, the luck of the age. There was a time when viral pneumonia wouldn't have kept either of us from our appointed rounds—rain, sleet, dark of night, when she and I had the hungers of the young."

"Bummer, Judge. I don't believe you. You just couldn't leave your work. Wouldn't. You should've gone."

"Well, whatever. Anyway, that's not why I called."

"Even bigger news?"

"I wanted to tell you there's no need to rush back to the City of Brotherly Love."

"They've closed it for the weekend."

"Ho, ho. The fact is, you'll be pleased to know, that once again, you've scrambled out of the briar patch into the rose garden."

"Bad metaphor, Judge, one thornfield to another."

"Now you grade my metaphors. Very well, let's say you've emerged from the swamp and come up *smelling* like a rose."

"Better. The Camilli case. Something broke with the state's witness."

"Never got that far. Early this morning the police picked up a suspect on a simple assault charge, and he proceeded to confess to no less than eleven crimes, large and small, including—"

"The murder of Esther Lewis!"

"Amazing what a skillful lawyer can do. As if you made the arrest yourself."

"I trust those vigilant watchdogs of the law at the PD paid heed to *Miranda* and—"

"Proper arrest, proper confession, everything tied up neatly."

Nick sighed with relief. "I knew Camilli was innocent. I just had to keep the case up in the air until something broke." Scattered on the night table next to him were the keys to his rental car, his wallet, money clip, and the shamrock from Julie. Nick picked up the shamrock and fondled it. "And I got lucky."

"Yes. I must say, you did a fine job as well, though I might have prepared a suitable lecture for you if that ploy with the wonder witness of the changed name had backfired."

"I had my bet covered."

"I imagine so. Anyway, if you hadn't sworn off gambling, I'd say *you* should be on your way to Atlantic City."

"I never so much swore off gambling as off losing."

"You're luckier at law."

"Yeah, lucky." He stared broodingly at the shamrock. "Careful's more like it. Careful and particular. Kind of guy'd buy dandruff insurance. Amazing how easy you can make your life if you're careful enough. Damn!" He flung the shamrock down onto the night table, it bounced up onto its edge and rolled off, dropped to the floor and came to rest leaning crazily against the table leg.

"What?"

"Nothing." Nick stared down at the shamrock as

if waiting for it to continue its performance. "Thanks for calling, Judge. I'll see you Monday."

"Monday? But I just told you—"

"I turned down the case here, Judge."

"Oh? Cut-and-dried guilty, for a local lawyer to handle?"

"As a matter of fact, I don't think he is guilty."

"Then what—"

"Just not my number. Tell you later. Good night, Judge." He hung up quickly before the judge could respond, and lay staring down at the shamrock. He would explain it all when he got back to Philadelphia.

Why not now, over the phone?

Because he wasn't comfortable with it somehow, with the explanation. He reached down for the shamrock and replaced it with his other pocket items. Either he would keep it or he would send it back; it wasn't his to throw away.

He dialed the desk and told them to hold his calls.

He folded his arms behind his head and stared at the ceiling. Christ, how he hated the mob. And he could hate anybody who, of free will, got involved with the syndicate just to have a nice life. So let the bastard hang.

How in hell could he have missed it there in the lawyer's room at the jail? Ordinarily he could pick up vibrations in a room like a bat nips insects in the air. He didn't feel it from Lon Braden. The wife—that was something else again. A wife doesn't have to know. Just blind, dumb loyalty. Maybe. But from Braden himself, nothing radiated that triggered Nick's nerve endings. Except that, for all his evasion, he seemed aware, complex, and oddly direct.

Maybe if they'd been given the full time together, Nick would have caught it, the mob mentality.

In any event, during the short time they had, Nick

had not picked it up. Braden had not seemed quite the type. He didn't whine, like a mob low-life; he didn't strike a macho pose. There was strength in his nervous tension, even independence. In his eyes. He was scared, but he was calculating at the same time. He hadn't seemed to welcome Nick as a representative from on high. He had seemed more like he was prepared to go it alone. Odd.

Nick hated the smell of the hotel room. He wrinkled up his nose and sniffed. He raised an arm and sniffed under it.

It was he that smelled. Christ, he had been too tired last night to take a shower! All day he had been pooping around in this room. Now it was almost bedtime again.

He swung off the bed and stripped off his clothes and plodded into the bathroom. He stood in the shower for a long time, lathering up again and again as if he could wash off his grouchy mood.

When he turned off the water, he thought he heard something. He listened, guessed he had been mistaken.

Then it came again—a light knock. Somebody was at the door.

Jesus H. Palooka, you tell them to hold your calls, they send somebody up.

He wrapped a towel around his waist and padded to the door. He opened it to see a tall, dark, heavy-set man in a shiny gray suit.

"Mr. Hellinger?"

"Yeah."

"Excuse me, but would you come with me, sir? Mr. Rossetti would like to see you in the dining room."

"Mr. Rossetti."

"Yes, sir."

"I don't know Mr. Rossetti."

"No, sir, but he knows you. It's important."

"Tell Mr. Rossetti he can see me on page seventeen of this week's *National Enquirer*—I'm a seer. Now I'm going beddy-bye."

Nick tried to shut the door, but the man blocked it firmly with his shoulder.

"Now, sir. Please. I'll wait while you get dressed."

Nick could ignore the man and just leave him standing there. But he didn't seem the type to go away. Nick could make noise. But he preferred to avoid that. The appointment was for the dining room—not a car ride.

So, what the hell, given the options, he would meet this Rossetti, and he would learn a little and remember it all. Including the face. Not a bad idea. They were not dealing with a pussycat here. He liked learning about them. Eventually he would have a lot of pieces, and he would put them together. Nick Hellinger would come back to haunt them.

So he put on a clean suit, stuffed his wallet and money clip into his pockets—adding, as an afterthought, the shamrock. He went out the door to follow the man to the dining room.

CHAPTER 4

IT HAD not occurred to him that the dining room would be closed, but he had really lost track of time. It was a large room, dimly lit, with chairs stacked upside down on tables like skeletons in an old burial ground. It was deserted except for one man sitting at a table in the rear, pointed out by the man who had led Nick down.

The man looked up from the table, beckoned to Nick. As Nick entered, two other men slipped in behind him but remained at the door—evidently to assure that they would not be disturbed. His guide now trailed him through the dining room to the occupied table.

Nick sized up his host as he approached. Around forty, dark-haired, wearing horn-rimmed glasses, trim, solid build, dark blue suit. In front of him was a white coffee cup, beside him a phone. Across from him was a place-setting with a wine glass, and alongside the chair an open wine bottle stood at a tilt in an ice bucket.

Offering a thin-lipped smile, the man said, "Mr. Hellinger? Bill Rossetti. Thanks for seeing me."

"Glad I could fit you in." He ignored Rossetti's extended hand. "Okay, Rossetti, I've seen you. I've also seen snakes in the Everglades. Maybe you've got a postcard of yourself I could take back to the kids. Don't I look thrilled?"

"Our files say you've got a weakness for vintage madeira." He gestured to the wine bucket, then to the chair opposite him. "Please."

"My weakness doesn't extend to spoiling good wine with bad company. If your files are accurate, you also know that I suffer fools badly, scoundrels not at all. You've got a pitch, Rossetti, make it fast. I left a seven-o'clock wake-up call, and I wouldn't want to miss Captain Kangaroo."

Rossetti did not flinch. He casually straightened his glasses on his nose. He had square, clean hands. "I understand you rejected Braden."

"Yeah. So?"

"We want you to take the case."

Nick grinned with narrowed eyes. "I'll bet you do."

"It's more important than you think."

"No it's not. I know just what it is. I may not be pretty, Rossetti, and I wasn't born in a manger. But I know, you lie down with goats, pretty soon you start to smell like one. The stink is unmistakable." He wrinkled his nose.

"At least listen—"

"I heard. You listen. You want to spring your boy, maybe you can try some kind of back-door play. I'm a front-door man." He started to turn away.

"We're prepared to pay you five hundred thousand dollars."

Nick turned back. "Use it to buy yourself a judge. You have trouble hearing, pal? I ain't a gun for hire, I ain't for sale. Make it simple—no."

Again Nick started away. The other man blocked him, putting a hand on his shoulder.

Nick looked down his nose at the hand. "Last man who did that is now known as Lefty."

Rossetti cleared his throat. "Mr. Hellinger."

Nick did not look back.

"I guess there's something you should see."

Now Nick turned to see Rossetti reaching into his jacket pocket. He took out a small fold-over wallet and slid it across the table.

Nick nodded. "Nice leather."

"Please."

He sighed, then stepped back to the table and picked up the wallet and opened it.

Credentials. Real. "Justice Department," Nick mumbled, stunned. "What the hell is . . . I figured you were part of—"

"You were supposed to. But our files are indeed accurate, and I could tell I had played out my string with you."

"You were right."

"So I had to open it up, bring you in." Rossetti shrugged. "Anyway, now you know. Please?" Again he motioned to the chair, and again Nick sat down. "I head a special team based here in the Southwest. A kind of strike force. At the moment we're attached to the U.S. Attorney's office here. You're familiar with how the U.S. Attorneys work, that should make it easier for you."

"Nothing here has the ring of easy to it." Nick lifted the bottle from the ice, checked the label, and sniffed at the top. "Hmm." He poured himself a glass.

Rossetti pushed the phone over to him. "Feel free to check me out."

"Oh, I will. In my own way." He sipped the wine and nodded. "Excellent. My compliments to your files. You were saying?"

"Clint Tolliver hasn't contacted you."

"No. Not directly, anyway. Unless you count Mrs. Braden."

"No, she's not part of it. But we expect that Tolliver isn't going to let you slip away without a dose of his, well, personal persuasion."

"Oh?"

"But we didn't know how quickly word would get back to him. He certainly thought you'd take the case. So he wouldn't move until he heard otherwise. And we were afraid you'd leave before he caught up with you."

"So you wanted him to get to me."

"Right. We were hoping he could convince you to take the case."

"You mean really? Actually defend Braden, spring him?"

"Right."

"For Tolliver, you wanted me to work."

"That's right."

"To get Braden free."

"Right."

"Why?"

"Because Alonzo Braden is one of us. He's our man inside the operation."

Nick had started to take another sip of wine, his

hand froze in midair. He gaped at Rossetti.

For the first time, Rossetti looked a little smug. "We've fooled a lot of people, Mr. Hellinger."

"I guess you better tell me about it."

Rossetti looked off. "It's a long story. Very long. I'll give you the outline. This has been a tough one all the way."

"Like I said, nothing here sounds easy."

Rossetti chuckled dryly. "I don't know what the word means anymore."

"I'm curious, Rossetti—just checking out my instincts. Did you put him in there, or did you just put the lock on him when he was in?"

"We put him in. He was ours all the way."

Nick nodded and smiled. "That makes me feel better. I didn't make him as mob type. Okay, so give."

Rossetti leaned back and folded his arms behind his head, staring pensively into the air. Then he leaned forward on his elbows. "You know how difficult it is to slip a guy into the Mafia? I mean really in?"

"I've got an idea."

"Well, you're right. I'd rather stick a pipe bomb in the President's lunch pail. It goes bad, not only do you lose your man, you lose your chance to get into that aspect of the operation until the next ice age."

"They know you're trying, all the time."

"Yeah. We keep mixing it up, as you know. On our side. Shuffling teams to keep new faces around, unknown faces. I was working southern Florida for a long time—Miami, the Beach, Lauderdale—working informants into the drug trade from South America. But for the last few years of that, I was still there, but I was working the beginnings of the operation here."

"How long ago?"

"Say four years. But it started way before that. Ten years ago we recruited Lon Braden off a university campus."

"Which one?"

"Don't grill me, okay? I'll tell you what you need to know. So, Braden had a distant cousin who was mobbed-up. It was an entree, and we had an urgent need to penetrate Tolliver's operation. He was going very big. Took us a while to hit on Braden, a while more to work him up, make sure."

"What made you sure, if I can ask that."

"Braden was clean, what we mean by clean. Nonpolitical, not active in any groups, not a big social cat. A quiet, conservative accounting student with top grades, a guy who seemed involved only with numbers. Kept to himself. Married already, stabile, anxious to make a good living."

"That's not enough."

"No. We had our eye on him for a while, just because of his cousin. And we picked up some signs."

"Such as?"

"Braden was tough in his quiet way. And honest. We put a man around him, he got to know him pretty well. Little things. After a while, Braden let it slip that he hated this distant cousin because of his involvement. But he never let the cousin know that. Kept it to himself. Himself and our man who became his friend. In time, he revealed himself to be more political than anybody knew. He had a powerful sense of right and wrong. But he didn't crow about it. He let people do whatever they did, made up his own mind. In short, he was the kind of guy who kept his mouth shut, did his work, didn't make waves, but had a passionate belief in the right things."

"Married, though. Probably not anxious to take big risks."

"Right and wrong. That was the way he seemed, all right. And that made him good for us. Because underneath those appearances, Lon Braden was a cooker."

"And the wife?"

"Extremely supportive, would go wherever we wanted, wouldn't question his motives. And once we got him interested, his demand was that she not know about his true status. Fine with us. That was our attitude exactly."

"So how'd you move him in?"

Rossetti shook his head. "The first part was easy—a long shot, but relatively easy. He applied for a job. Made it known that he had applied for several. His pitch was he wanted to make money. He didn't care about anything else. And there was a lot of new, promising money in the Houston area. Place was booming, gonna be hot. He made a hard pitch for money. That got Tolliver interested."

"I do not suppose that Tolliver is dumb."

Rossetti grinned. "Dumb enough. Like so many mobsters. Brighter than a laser in some ways. But narrow-beamed like that too. Blind to the sides. Their weakness is that they think they're so damned smart. Anyway, he was smart enough to have Braden checked out. I mean thoroughly. He liked that he had a cousin already connected. And he didn't find anything wrong. Braden was married, wife pregnant. Guy like that couldn't arouse too many suspicions, and wouldn't want to bring trouble down on his head. Tolliver topped the best previous offer Braden had got. He moved to Houston, went to work."

"Been there a long time."

"Whew, you're telling me. It's been slow going. Frustrating. Walking on eggshells all the way. Nerve-wracking. A lesser guy would have ducked and run.

But he hung in. Steel, the guy is. For eight years, Braden stuck to Tolliver like white on rice, earning his trust, working himself into a position of responsibility."

"Good accountant." Nick nodded.

"The best, for Tolliver's purposes. But eight years, *eight years!* And during that time we don't get enough to fill a postcard. Sometimes we even got suspicious ourselves. What the hell was he doing? Just making a lot of money? He was patient as an ox. We had to be too. Then, suddenly, the sluice-gates opened. Bonanza! Names, dates, confidential information tied to mob activities all over the country!"

"You struck it rich."

Rossetti leaned closer. "What Braden's been feeding us the past two years is beyond price, and he's fed it to us, Mr. Hellinger, knowing that the slightest slip . . ." Rossetti drew a finger across his throat.

"Likewise for his wife."

"Well, they don't ordinarily like to touch wives, as you know. But in this case, at least from Braden's viewpoint, yeah, he had to be thinking about that. And his daughter."

"You got your information, maybe it's time he packed it in."

"We kicked that around. He was getting nervous, but he had them by the throat. He wanted to hang in a little longer."

"Maybe you shouldn't have left it up to him. You could've pulled him."

"You don't bench the star quarterback in the middle of the Super Bowl."

"Of course not. Just tape his ribs, shoot him full of cortisone, and send him back onto the field."

Rossetti was quiet for a few moments, contemplating Nick's frown. Then he said, "Look, a couple of months from now the Senate will be conducting hearings into the infiltration of legitimate businesses by organized crime. I'm not talking about your local laundry or car wash. I'm talking about giant corporations listed on the major stock exchanges. I'm talking about oil supertankers with Panamanian registries and mob ownership. I'm talking about shopping malls"—he tapped his finger on the table as he ticked them off—"and sports arenas and amusement parks that have come into being because certain elected officials are on the syndicate payroll."

"You're talking about a lot."

"Yeah. And Braden's almost got his end of it wrapped up. Almost. So you weigh all that against the safety of one man..."

"One man's expendable. Never mind he's got a wife and kid."

"Tolliver's operation is costing lives all down the line." Rossetti fixed him with a hard look. "Braden's a foot soldier. I need him back on the firing line. It's as simple as that."

"You're all heart, Rossetti."

"It's a rough business."

"So now, I just get him acquitted, no matter how, right?"

"Right."

"So he can get back to work and tidy up all the little stories."

"It wasn't our idea to hire you, Hellinger. But we were pleased with the choice."

"I love compliments. I was the guy to find the loopholes."

"We know what you can do."

"Forgive a dumb question, but do you believe he's innocent?"

"Want an honest answer?"

"Give it a try."

"We don't know, we don't care. It looked like Paul Savage was going to blow Braden's cover."

"Where'd Savage get it? That must have worried you."

"Are you kidding? We scattered like ants, looking for the source. We figured it must have come out of Washington, a leak from some Senator's office. But now we don't think so. We don't think Savage had anything solid. Fishing expedition, lot of names floating around. Virtually everybody close to Tolliver. But we didn't have time to nail it down. Savage was looking like he was going to go with it."

"Just a little too late for him, and Braden."

"For everybody. But you got to understand Savage. He would go with it even if he didn't know shit for sure. The fact that he might be signing a man's death warrant didn't even faze him. He had a hot scoop, the kind of headline-grabber that could catapult a regional TV journalist into network prime time." Rossetti lowered his head. "Obviously, he had to be stopped."

"Oh, obviously."

Rossetti shook his head. "Braden should've let me know what he was up to. I guess he figured there wasn't time. But if he'd have clued me, we'd have taken care of it."

Nick leaned close to him, nose to nose. "How do I know you didn't?"

Rossetti gave him a half-smile. "I guess you don't, counselor."

Nick shoved his chair back and stood up. "I got an early flight, Rossetti."

"You can't just walk away from this, not now."

"Is that a threat, G-man?" He turned, eyed the other man out of his way, and left.

No, he didn't know. There was sure as hell a lot of stuff he didn't know. Take it from the top: he didn't even know if Alonzo Braden was a murderer or not. He didn't know who Braden was. He didn't know who Rossetti was. Only Tolliver, whom he had not yet met, could he feel reasonably sure he knew; and that because the DA hadn't been lying.

The stuff of another sleepless night. He lay awake for a short time, then had to get out of the damn hotel room; he felt he had been there forever.

It wasn't really all that late for a Saturday night, though most places were closed. He wanted a drink, a place where he might just idly listen to conversation without having to make any.

He pulled open the door to a place called Bunkey's that looked all right. Middle-of-the-road, not a dive, not a biker's bar, not a singles' hangout—ordinary. It had a few tables with large green lights hanging over them, and in the back a small pool table with a green light over that. Nobody was at the pool table. A couple of tables were occupied. Two men sat at one end of the bar, a man and woman sat in the middle. Nick took a seat at the other end.

"Suh?" the bartender said, wiping his hands with a towel. He had a mustache and suspenders, and the first Texas accent Nick could remember hearing in Houston.

"Double Chivas on the rocks."

The bartender took down the squat bottle, fished somewhere below the counter for ice, and poured the drink. He dropped a round cork coaster on the counter in front of Nick and put the drink on the coaster.

"Thanks."

"Yes, suh."

He took a good slug of the scotch, felt it warm his gullet.

The man and woman a few stools from his stared down at their drinks. The man mumbled something. The woman said, "It doesn't matter what you say."

Not a good start; Nick wanted mindless, barroom chatter to take his mind off business.

A woman slid onto the stool next to him. She didn't look at him. Tight dress, cleavage, well-tanned, tiny gold chains around her neck and wrists, golden half-moon earrings. Dark blond hair with lighter streaks, pulled back and tied with a purple ribbon. Nice nose, pudgy cheeks, full lips glossed orange, eyes lidded purple. Not bad.

"Ma'am?" the bartender asked, wiping his hands.

The woman now looked at Nick, smiling around small teeth. "Would you like to buy me a drink?"

Nick cocked an eyebrow, chuckled under his breath. After a pause, he said, "Sure, why not?"

"Harvey Wallbanger," she said to Nick with "r's" hard enough to be Chicago.

The bartender waited politely for Nick to repeat the order, which he did.

She didn't look at him again until her drink had been served. She arranged it carefully in front of her, her hands turning the coaster just so. She took a sip, then turned to him. "Well, what's on your mind?"

"Trying to get things off it."

"Hmm." She took another sip. "Anything I can do to help?"

"Who knows?"

"I mean, would you like to talk or anything."

"I'm in a listening mood."

"Oh. Well, I've been taking a walk. It's a nice night." She touched an earring. "Nice way to get your mind off things. What's your name?"

"Alex."

"Mine's Esmeralda. But my friends call me Pooch." She fingered the chains at her neck, let her hand slide down to the cleavage. It stayed there. "Warm in here, don't you think, Alex?"

Nick was tempted. He hadn't been looking, hadn't been thinking about it. It had been a long time since he'd been tempted in a bar. Longer since he'd been tempted by a pro. Pooch, for chrissake. He just wanted to relax. "Hey, Pooch." He smiled and covered her hand on the counter with his.

"Yes, Alex?"

"Who you working for, sugar?"

"What?"

His grip tightened, so did his smile. "You're too slick to just walk off the street into a place like this, baby. And you ain't Miss Lonelyheart either."

"What are you talking about?" She tried to withdraw her hand.

"Somebody wants me to hang around, Pooch lady. You'd be one way. But I deal direct."

"I don't know what you're talking about. I think I'd better leave."

"Naw, naw." He loosed her hand. "Finish your drink."

She drained it.

"Now leave."

He watched her stalk out. He could have been wrong. But he could smell a net a mile away. And she had a distinct fishy odor.

That didn't make it easier to sleep, but at least it killed a little more of the night. With the East Coast time difference, he could get busy early in the morning.

So naturally he overslept. It was after ten when he finally got his eyes open, almost eleven by the time he got down to the dining terrace.

The terrace adjoining the main dining room was crowded, which suited his purpose just fine. The babble of voices around him gave him privacy. The sun was brilliant. A humid breeze ruffled the napkin under his coffee cup.

He cradled the phone on his shoulder to sip his coffee while he waited for the information he had requested. When it came, he jotted the number on a small legal pad. "Yeah, I got it. Thanks for the phone number, Lew. I'll drop by the next time I'm in Washington. By then I'll be able to explain the whole mess. Owe you one. Ta-ta."

He sipped his coffee and dialed another number. It rang several times. Then when it was picked up, there was a pause before the male voice: "Yes?"

"Mr. Langley," Nick said without hesitating, "my name is Nick Hellinger. I'm an attorney from Philadelphia. I'm in Houston right now."

"I know who you are, Mr. Hellinger," the voice drawled, "and where. How did you get this number?"

"A friend in a high place." Douglas Langley was the assistant U.S. Attorney for this Texas jurisdiction. Langley was probably not so surprised that Nick could get his home phone number as he was that Nick was doing this his own way. "Last night, a man came to see me. Five-ten, dark curly hair, wears horn-rimmed glasses that I couldn't tell if they were real or window glass—"

"Bill Rossetti."

"That's what he called himself."

"Right. He's on my staff, Mr. Hellinger. Very

perceptive about the glasses. He tells me you turned down the Braden case."

"Yeah."

"But that you're reconsidering, in light of what he told you."

"He took a lot for granted, Mr. Langley, but he guessed right."

"You're going to take it?"

"Yeah. Rossetti is Rossetti, I'll take the part of Hellinger."

"I'm relieved. He will be too. So will Braden."

"I don't feel relieved. Very dicey circumstances, Mr. Langley."

"We've been living with it a long time."

"Yeah, well, you'll be alive no matter what."

Langley was silent for a few seconds. "What's your next move, Mr. Hellinger?"

"I haven't told anybody yet. I'm waiting for Tolliver himself to convince me. Otherwise my sudden change of heart's going to smell like yesterday's flounder. Rossetti did not make me feel good."

"You haven't been approached by Tolliver yet?"

"No, not directly. But I'm wearing a sports jacket and tie, very Philadelphia. I won't be hard to find. I hope somebody connects soon, I'm on my fifth cup of coffee. I feel a hum inside."

"We have a lot of respect for you, Mr. Hellinger, and we're depending on you. You think there's a shot at bail?"

"Oh, sure. Murder one. A note from his parents will do it."

"Well, maybe you'll come up with something. We want you to get him out, that's all."

"That's not quite all, Mr. Langley, not anymore.

77

There's also the minor matter of being a double agent, not letting anything slip about what I know, not having anybody link me to Rossetti, or you—you know, secrecy and all that jazz. Not that I'm complaining, mind you. It's all very exciting."

Another pause from Langley. "We're not unaware of the high demands of this matter on you, Mr. Hellinger. But we are depending on you."

"I'll do my best. Don't be surprised if—uh-oh . . ."

Leo, the limousine driver, was standing in the dining-room doorway looking around. He was not wearing his uniform, but a conservative, dark-blue suit. It transformed him; he was not, it seemed, just an ignorant lackey.

Nick lowered his voice. "Looks like the Gulf Coast Godfather's sent his boy."

"Leo."

"You got it."

"Good."

"Marvelous. Later." Nick hung up as Leo approached the table.

"Mr. Hellinger?"

Nick took a sip of coffee and looked up innocently.

"Remember me, sir? I picked you and Mrs. Braden up at the airport."

"Yeah."

"I drive for Mr. Tolliver."

"Oh, yes. How's the family?"

"I'm not married. But personally, I'm—"

"Forget it. We going somewhere?"

"I hope you don't mind helicopters."

"Naw, some of my best friends are choppers. Let's go."

Leo was a somber, solid man who seemed accustomed to not intruding but was politely responsive. He was the kind of man, Nick thought, who would unquestioningly do whatever asked by his boss, the kind of man such a boss would trust. There was no point in trying to pump him, and Nick was not interested in casual conversation with a gorilla.

So the ride to the airport and in the helicopter was fairly mute. But Leo was not any ordinary gorilla; he flew the chopper himself. Nick wondered if he was the right age to have learned it in Vietnam. Hard to figure Leo's age. What he had thought were simple creases across his forehead were in fact scars, Nick noticed when he had a chance to look him over in the chopper, and they could have come from Vietnam or a back alley in Houston.

The Texas countryside wobbled beneath the thumping, bobbing bubble. They gradually moved away from the oil country and grasslands around Houston and over the cotton and cattle country to the northwest. The landscape now was brown and not so flat.

Nick leaned over to Leo and called above the thump of the rotor, "How long to Tolliver's ranch?"

Leo angled his head toward him without looking at him. "We've been over it for about ten minutes."

Nick saw the buildings that would be houses and barns. They dropped down and took one lower sweep around over a corral where there were several people and a few horses. Then they hovered and sank slowly onto a concrete landing pad a hundred yards from the main house, a low, rambling, Spanish-style mansion.

A couple of men wearing "CT" caps trotted over, ducking under the rotor as it whined to a stop. They said nothing as Leo and Nick debarked, then they set about tending to the chopper.

Leo led Nick not toward the house but further on toward the corral. A couple of dozen people were scattered around the fence, or sitting on it, some wearing business suits, some ranch-hand gear, all wearing ten-gallon hats.

On the far side, suddenly a gate opened and a black bucking horse charged out, and the crowd cheered. Aboard the horse was a boy perhaps thirteen or fourteen, one gloved hand gripping the cinch in front of the saddle, the other waving wildly in the air. The horse kicked and whirled, the boy's spurs flashed back and forth along the flanks.

One husky voice rose above the rest: "Hang in there, T.J.! Dig in! Lay back! You got the rhythm now! Weight inside on the spin! You got him—"

The boy's hat went flying, his head was snapped wickedly forward and back. Abruptly the horse reversed its spin, heaved the other way. The boy clung for a moment at an awkward angle, then was tossed.

Groans and gasps came from the crowd. The boy rolled over in the dust. He lay on his back for a few seconds, then sat up. Getting his bearings, he hopped to his feet and walked toward the fence, rubbing his backside.

"Helluva ride, T.J.! You'll get him next time!"

Now Nick could see the man with the husky voice. There was no mistaking his dominance of the scene. Heads turned toward him and nodded, voices echoed his.

That would have to be him. A formidable, barrel-chested, ruddy-faced man in a white Stetson with a bright feather in the band, a magnificent fringed suede jacket, and lizard-skin boots; the man had at least a grand in the outfit alone.

Clearly he was aware of their arrival. As soon as the boy walked away from the horse, the man turned toward Leo and Nick as they approached. Flint eyes, a broad smile that didn't soften them.

He ignored Leo and stuck his hand out to Nick. "Mr. Hellinger, I'm Clint Tolliver. I appreciate your coming."

Nick resisted the temptation to match Tolliver's grip, letting his hand be squeezed by the larger one of Tolliver's. They were about the same height. Nick wondered what kind of shape the man was in. The kind of man who counted on destroying you with the first punch or two.

By signal or prearrangement, a nappy gray Stetson was passed to Tolliver, and he offered it to Nick.

"Sun's pretty bright out here." He winked at Nick's bald pate.

Nick hesitated, then put it on. He felt ridiculous.

"Not so far back." Tolliver tugged the front brim down. "There you go."

Nick peered under the lowered brim of the hat, nodding toward the corral. "Good show. Who's winning?"

"So far, the horse." Tolliver put a hand on his back and steered him along past the onlookers. "Tarbaby, wise old bastard. Not an easy one to learn on. But he'll teach you."

"Not me. I'm strictly a spectator."

Tolliver chuckled, the sound of a cement mixer. "You fancy the noblest breed, Mr. Hellinger?"

"The running kind. In my day, I've made many a bookmaker wealthy beyond his wildest dreams."

Tolliver's chuckle rumbled again. "Now, that's a whole nother ballgame, whole nother kind of education."

Dust blew up, Nick rubbed his eyes.

"You'll get used to that. Good, clean Texas air, comes with the finest grit. Come on, maybe you'd like to meet a few of the folks around the fence here."

Nick halted. "Mr. Tolliver..."

"Please, it's Clint."

"Yeah. Well, I may not look busy, but I am. I've already wasted two days looking for a yellow rose in this state, and everything's coming up weeds. Your boy said you wanted to talk business. So let's talk."

"Sure, certainly. I just thought we'd get comfortable, let you kind of settle in gradual. We like to make things comfortable in these parts."

"I'm on Philly time—that's as in city, not horse. I'm comfortable enough."

"That a fact?" Tolliver gave him a lopsided smile, like he was going to pick his teeth. "Well then, let's talk."

Tolliver altered his course away from the corral. Leo fell in behind them at a respectful distance just out of earshot.

"Well, I'll tell you," Tolliver said quietly, like a parson, "I'll make no bones about it, Lon Braden is more than just an ordinary employee to me. I care about all of my employees, of course. Protect 'em when they need it, defend 'em when there's trouble around. Even if they're wrong, they know they got me to lean on . . ."

"Braden's more," Nick urged him on.

"You bet. Been with me for years. Never been any trouble, never been *in* any trouble. Clean as a spaceman." He looked at Nick. "You get a chance to see any of that space stuff down there in Houston?"

"No, no. So?"

"Lon Braden's bright, honest, loyal, trustworthy—"

"Brave, clean, and reverent." Nick held up three fingers. "I've defended a lot of Boy Scouts."

Tolliver frowned slightly, looking down at his lizard boots like a buzzard over a kill. "More than that, more than that. He's almost like a son to me."

"I'm a lawyer, Tolliver, not a family counselor."

"Please, Clint, hunh?" Tolliver put a hand on Nick's shoulder. Nick resisted the urge to shrug it off, but it wasn't easy. "He didn't kill that muckraker."

"Is that so?"

"Damn straight."

"How do you know that?"

"I believe Lon Braden. And I know him. He's not a killer. Not a violent bone in his body. Can't stomach it. Why, he can't even watch when we geld a stallion. But that's not all."

"Tell me what's more."

"He had no *reason* to kill that slimy bastard—not that a lot of people didn't have. I can't say it broke *my* heart neither, he got bumped. But Braden had no reason. Oh, I heard the rumors. But there's nothing to them. Nothing at all. Whole thing would've just blown right over, except for the multi million-dollar lawsuit I would've brought that would have shut his mouth forever on the airwaves."

"Let's cut the crap, shall we?" Now Nick put a hand on Tolliver's shoulder. "You've talked to Braden's wife. She told you why I refused the case."

"Yeah, but I don't buy it, altogether. According to what I know, you ain't a particular holier-than-thou type."

"I'm no saint, and by and large I don't defend saints. Saints tend to keep their hands out of the cookie jar and their pokers off other people's heads. But it's a funny thing—you go to work for the mob, before you know it the mob's your sole employer."

"Hey, now—"

"I don't like my shots being called by somebody

else, Tolliver. I like a varied clientele—I'm kind of a free lance that way. Keeps the creative juices flowing."

"Hold on now, just a minute. We don't have to go throwing around words like 'mob' and that. All right? This here's a big business I run—diversified, like you. And, you know, there's a little of this, little of that. But 'mob,' that's for TV and that. Okay?"

"Yeah, yeah." Nick kicked at the dust and was rewarded with another plume that assaulted his eyes. "So maybe it's all tooth-fairies you got. Just so we understand each other."

"That's better." Tolliver smiled with straight lips. "We understand each other."

"And to further complete that understanding, let me tell you something about myself. The ponies notwithstanding, I can afford to be choosy. Hellinger's Law: Choosy now, good choices later."

"Well now, just how choosy might you be able to afford to be?"

"Very."

Tolliver narrowed his eyes pensively, making them glinty streaks. "I'm not so good with words as I am with numbers."

"Not long ago I turned down five hundred thousand dollars under very similar circumstances."

"Half a mill—that's downright choosy."

"Yeah. And I never felt a twitch."

Tolliver cocked his head and smiled like a magician hiding something in his cheek. "I like a man doesn't twitch easy. I like a man like that a lot. Numbers are better for me. So I'll double that—one million, one whole one, in advance. Hunh? In any currency. To be deposited in your name in any country in the world. Now, that's because I'm choosy too, maybe choosier than you. And I choose you. Now how choosy are you?"

Nick smiled, lowering his eyelids. "I'm not a fanatic."

"So then, can I take it that our understanding's complete?"

Maintaining his stolid smile, Nick looked directly into Tolliver's eyes. "Yeah. Complete."

Tolliver responded with a pleasant show of teeth and clapped Nick on the back. "Sir, you are a man of enormous good sense."

"I'm complimented." They shook hands.

"Like to see some horses?"

"Why not? Maybe after this matter, I'll retire to stud."

"Well, you know, you have interests along that line, we can take care of that for you too."

"I have interests, but for the time being I better concentrate on being a lawyer. This is no easy case."

"Hence the fee."

"Exactly."

They walked toward the stables, Leo still trailing behind them.

"I'm reminded of a story," Tolliver said in a musing fashion. "Somehow I think it's appropriate."

"I'm all ears."

"It seems God was out strolling around the south forty and He came to the fence that separates the pastures of heaven from the scorched plains of hell. Much to His dismay, the fence was falling apart. God called the Devil over and said, 'Look here, this won't do. It's your responsibility to maintain this fence.' The Devil replied, 'I changed my mind.' The Lord said, 'I beg your pardon, do you intend to renege on our bargain?' The Devil said, 'Yup, I'm out.' The

Lord said, 'Then you'll be hearing from my lawyer in the morning!'"

Nick stopped him with a hand. "Whereupon Satan said, 'Now, *I've* got plenty of lawyers over here. But where are *you* going to find one?'"

Pique flashed in Tolliver's eyes. "You've heard it, then."

"Palermo, Sicily, nineteen-sixty-nine," Nick said, deadpan. "And would you believe from an even bigger crook than you."

"I am not a crook."

"We had a President said that once."

"So?"

"But it's still a good line."

CHAPTER 5

NICK PREPARED carefully for his next session with Lon Braden, poring over police reports and newspaper clippings, every once in a while leaving the table and lying down on his bed to stare at the ceiling and mull things over. In his mind, he pulled it apart, put it back together, sifted through the facts, rearranged them.

In another tough case like this, Nick might have attempted various delays and postponements to allow himself time to develop the defense. But in this case, the more time that passed, the more chance that something could go wrong. He didn't want delays. He wanted the case to go to trial. And he didn't have a defense, not yet.

After spending most of the day studying, he met with Braden in the lawyer's room at the jail.

That was grueling too. Nick didn't just walk in and tell Braden everything at once. The Justice Department had decided against the risks of trying to pass the word to Braden, so that left it all to Nick to lead Braden carefully, step by step, to the truth about what he was doing, what he knew. Only then could they get to the matter of the murder.

Nick removed his jacket which was streaked with sweat, and loosened his tie. Braden chain-smoked and paced—except when they were talking about his government role, during which times Braden sat across from Nick at the table and leaned close to him and spoke in a low voice. The ashtray was overflowing with cigarette butts. Nick jotted notes on a legal pad, which was soon nearly filled. Near him lay a copy of the *Houston Herald*.

Nick closely questioned Braden on every detail leading up to his discovery of the body, making him go over it again and again.

"Don't you believe me?" Braden complained from time to time.

Nick patiently explained that he did, but that was not the point. The point was to get the facts precisely, unshakably right.

"Now,"—Nick leaned back and tapped the pad with his pen—"I want to know how you felt when you were on your way to Savage's."

"How I felt? What the hell's that got to do with it?"

"Motive, my friend. It's going to come up. Let's get it straight right now. The truth."

"Okay, okay." Braden paced and nodded. "I was angry, sure I was angry when I went over there. That's putting it mildly. Hell, I was on fire! Would I have killed him? No. Probably not. But I was going to have to shut him up, whatever it took. I won't lie to you, Nick, finding him already dead didn't exactly bring a lump to my throat."

Nick was struck by how good a man Justice had picked. Tough and dedicated, no lightweight. "You heard voices, and a lamp crashing to the floor."

"Right—well, I didn't actually hear the lamp. I saw it go out, then I found it smashed."

"You missed the killer by seconds."

"Yeah, and he had to go over the back wall. That's the only way he could've got out of there without me spotting him."

"You told this to the arresting officers?" Nick knew that from the reports, but he wanted to keep Braden's memory right in sequence.

He nodded. "They advised me of my rights, and I told them the truth—except for why I was there, why I really was there. I thought maybe if I told them what I heard and so on right away, they'd go after the killer. But they figured I was it."

"Think about the room now, Savage's study. Think again. Any little detail you might have missed before."

"Oh, Christ." Braden sighed helplessly. "We've gone over this so many times."

"Think, man. Among other things we're dealing with here, it's your life."

"Jesus, my mind's an omelet . . ." He lit another cigarette, stamped it out among the others mechanically without smoking it. "I don't know . . . I seem to remember—shit, I'm not even sure I remember . . . a humming." He looked pleadingly over at Nick, as if for help. "Some kind of humming."

"The telephone. You said it was off the hook."

"Yeah, but I mean *after* I hung it up. There were the sirens, but I remember... I thought the phone was humming, but then I hung it up, and still..."

"Still the humming."

"Yeah, I think. Like the sound a movie projector makes, you know? But I'm not even sure about that now. I heard the police sirens and took off." He shrugged, smiled ruefully. "Or tried to, anyway."

Nick unfolded the newspaper, opening up the front page. He tapped his finger on the photograph. "From the looks of you, they were none too gentle with you."

Braden bent over the table to look at the photo, which showed him looking bedraggled as he was hauled along between two uniformed cops. "Oh, that. Wasn't the cops. It's the sprinklers that did that. Some rainbirds were on in Savage's backyard. I tripped over one and landed in the mud."

Nick made a note. "They didn't mistreat you in any way?"

"Naw, you can forget that route. They just took me in. I mean, they cuffed me, cuffed my wrists, but that's all. They were okay."

Nick leaned back in his chair, yawned, and stretched.

"We about done?" Braden asked. "I'm exhausted."

"Yeah. About."

"You got more to ask? Nick, I don't *know* any more."

"Mmm." Nick flipped back through the pages of his pad. "Question I haven't asked, and you can answer."

"Whew! Shoot."

"How did you know for sure that Savage was going to expose you?"

Braden sat quickly down, leaned over to Nick, folded his hands under his chest. "I was never absolutely sure. I knew he'd been checking me out. Apparently he put together a profile on anyone who was even remotely connected to Clint Tolliver's inner circle of employees. See, Tolliver's name has been just below the surface for a long time—rumors, newspaper guys nosing around, that sort of thing. People sort of thought they knew something, but nobody dared say anything because nobody could really get a handle on it. Plus they were scared. Tolliver would sue their asses blue, or worse. So that kind of stuff never worried me until lately."

"The Senate got involved."

"That's it." Braden nodded briskly. "It was like the home stretch, you know? Well, we're not dumb, we figured there might be leaks. You know, you get three, four Senators, their aides, everybody looking for a leg up on publicity, somebody's gonna leak something about what's coming up, even if they don't know what they're talking about. So it got rumored around that they were gonna nail Tolliver."

"And Savage got into it."

"Yeah, but that wasn't the problem. Savage wasn't as brave as he sounded, or as clean either. He was a parasite, amoral. No, he wasn't going to pick up the leak about Tolliver and run with it any more than the other weak-kneed journalists around here. He wasn't going to put himself on the line with a scoop about Tolliver and have Tolliver on his ass. No, Savage decided that the government must have somebody working inside the operation. Didn't take brilliance to come up with that, that's standard procedure, to have a snitch inside. Naturally, that's the way you make a case. So what was Savage going to do? Rather than help expose Tolliver, or even say the Senate was going to topple him, he was going to find the government's inside man and expose *him!*"

"Nice."

"Yeah, hunh? Real public service. Come on like a muckraking journalist while he was really going to screw up the investigation of Tolliver, give Tolliver a chance to clean up his act . . ."

"Meaning, get the snitch."

"Right. So he'd have the scoop, and he'd have Tolliver as a silent friend for life. Somebody in Washington handed it to Savage—at least that's the way I got it."

"Rossetti says they checked it out, they don't think Savage really had anything."

"I know. *Now* I know. But it didn't make any difference. Savage was going to name me. He was just taking a wild shot—what'd he have to lose? He'd name me, then somebody else inside, then somebody else. But meanwhile, he's made the headlines, he's alerted Tolliver, I'm gone." Braden scowled. "Or maybe something else?"

"What else?"

"I'm the guy with the books, I handle the numbers. Maybe Savage figures I'm the guy he can tap into for a nice, big payoff, to buy him off the story."

Nick cocked his head. "Spell it out."

"The morning before the night Savage was killed, I walk into the office and my secretary hands me a message from Savage suggesting I catch his show that night. Nobody had to draw me a picture. Alonzo Braden, CPA, is not normally big news, right? I figured he'd hit paydirt. I tried to reach him, but he wouldn't take my calls. He wasn't at the station when I went there, his assistant didn't want me to find him.

What was I supposed to do? I was going nuts! If he'd have gone on the air with that story, I'd be snuffed before the first commercial—let alone what might happen to my family."

"But if he didn't have the story, if he was just looking for a payoff from you, he would have wanted you to reach him."

"Unless he was going to let me sweat through that broadcast, taunt me with it without naming me, then threaten to do it the next week for real. That would really bring me to my knees, right? Let me stew a while, go completely crazy with fear. I'd give him anything he wanted. Why else would he tip me to watch the broadcast, other than to get me squirming?"

"But if he didn't have anything on you, if he didn't think you were the government source, why would he think you'd come across?"

"Because either way, Nick, all he had to do was suggest it on the air, Tolliver would make me disappear—I mean in small pieces. Savage knew that. He knew there was no way I could convince Tolliver he was wrong. So he knew I'd come across whether I was the guy or not. I wouldn't have had a chance."

"So when you went to Savage's . . ."

"I had to know whether he had something for real, or he was just putting the squeeze on me. Either way he had to be stopped."

"Why didn't you let Rossetti handle it?"

Braden shook his head. "There wasn't time. We're talking about a couple of hours. When you're working inside like I am, Nick, you gotta be prepared to take emergency measures on your own. That's the business."

"Yeah. And the business isn't finished."

"Nick, I'm scared about the trial."

"I won't let them convict you."

"Not that. But if there's a leak, the slightest slip that gives me away..."

"That won't happen either. I won't let it happen." He gave Braden's shoulder a squeeze. Then he rose from the table and gathered up his papers. "I didn't travel all this distance just to get a suntan. And I'm not staying for my health."

Braden smiled grimly and stuck out his hand. They were in it together now, the trust was a two-way street.

There was, of course, a prior attorney of record who had put in the initial appearance for Braden, Nick assumed it was one of those quiet firms nobody heard much about. For his ordinary service down here, Tolliver wouldn't have a noise-maker. These lawyers would be Tolliver's handymen. It was nothing new for Nick to be called into a case under such circumstances, and he wasn't worried about asserting himself—clearly Tolliver wanted him running things.

But when he faced the press, he preferred to do it alone. He had his own effective style. Tolliver's lackeys could have scheduled the conference in Nick's hotel, out of deference to him. Maybe this other hotel was more the law-firm's turf, or maybe it was just where the press was used to meeting people down here. Just as well; Nick didn't want to draw all that much attention to where he was staying.

He was not on time. He was going to have to play the press a little differently in this case. He wanted them respectful, not necessarily friendly. He was, after all, working for Clint Tolliver.

He strode through the lobby and took the elevator to the third floor. As he stepped out, a young man with curly, close-cropped hair, large innocent eyes, and a pinstriped suit came quickly forward.

"Mr. Hellinger? I'm Andy Clay. I'm a junior associate with Graebner, Wilkes, and Cassellman."

"Ah..."

"They're waiting for you in the conference room."

Nick shook the young man's hand. "Reporters growing surly, are they?"

"Well, they *have* been waiting, and you *are* the star attraction."

They moved down the corridor.

"Mrs. Braden here?" Nick asked.

"In fact, she is, we were surprised."

"I asked her to come. She's a very sympathetic figure."

"Good idea. Sometime, if you've got the time, I'd like to discuss the Delgado case with you, Mr. Hellinger."

"The Delgado case?" Nick looked at him, surprised. "Why that one? I was shot down in flames."

"By a technicality!" Clay jabbed a finger in the air. "It was the most brilliantly organized defense I've ever read. If the judge hadn't barred testimony from—"

"Yeah, yeah, if." Nick smiled. This Clay was not just another button-down law grad with dreams of a blue-chip stock portfolio. The Delgado case indeed. An obscure larceny case that Nick had in fact argued brilliantly. Good case for a young lawyer to study. If Andrew Clay wanted to impress him, he couldn't have picked a better example.

They came to the door of the conference room, Nick stopped him with a hand. "By the way, I won that case on appeal." Without waiting for his reaction, Nick pushed the door open and went in ahead.

The meeting room was jammed with press. Behind the table sat Cara Braden and three men older than Hellinger. Three soft-looking men in dark suits, one man with black hair combed straight back, one with a stubble of gray hair, one with wavy white hair and a florid face.

It was the last who got up and welcomed Nick to the table, giving him a mechanical smile and limp handshake and introducing himself as Henry Graebner.

Nick gave Cara a quick hug and sat down next to her. He saw Andy Clay move to the back of the room to watch. Intelligent. Back there you could hear the side comments of newsmen.

Nick whispered to Cara, "You okay?"

"They're like hyenas."

"Yeah, they think they've really got something to feed on here. But they haven't. Don't worry. This is the fun part."

Graebner stood at the lectern and smiled into the cameras.

"Well, gentlemen, I thank you for being so patient . . ."

Nick sighed. First the old klutz had to foist it off on him, for being late, putting a little distance between the locals and the foreigner.

". . . but now we can begin. The firm of Graebner, Wilkes, and Cassellman is proud to be joined in this defense by one of the country's premier—" He laughed a light, cocktail-party laugh and bowed to Nick. "Excuse me, counselor, *the* premier criminal attorney, the eminent Nicholas Hellinger."

Nick nodded without smiling.

"And now," Graebner said like a professor concluding a lecture, "any questions you may have." He sat down.

A voice from the back: "What brought you down here, Mr. Hellinger? The case or the money?"

Nick let a moment pass, then lazily got to his feet and stepped to the lectern. He scanned the press corps with hooded eyes. "Did I hear a question?"

The questioner stood, pencil poised over his pad as if he were about to harpoon it. "Dave Fredericks, *Houston Herald,* Mr. Hellinger." His tone was more deferential now. "What I meant was—"

"I heard the question, Mr. Fredericks. Fair enough, for starters. To answer it, let me say first that I believe Alonzo Braden to be innocent."

"Well, naturally, but what I—"

"And second, my fee is immaterial." He gave them time to note his words. "Unless, of course, you believe that the higher the fee, the better the defense." He enjoyed watching their heads pop back up, and smiled broadly. "In which case, this will be my finest hour."

He could sense Mrs. Braden tense behind him, but she would just have to get used to it. In the back, Andy Clay smiled, and Nick liked that.

Other reporters jumped up and began asking questions at the same time.

"Are you aware of allegations of Braden's connections with . . ."

"Is Clint Tolliver paying your fee?"

"Was Savage's death related to his anticrime series?"

"Fellas!" Nick held out his arms benedictorily. "One at a time, hunh?"

A young blond man in a chino leisure suit folded

his arms over his chest—he would be a TV reporter: "Will Braden's alleged mob affiliations be an issue in this trial?"

"Are *you* alleging that?"

"Well, there have been—"

"You, friend, can make any assumptions you want. The charge is murder. I can't tell you what the prosecution may attempt to bring in. I can only tell you that the DA's office would be advised to stick to the facts—you too."

Fredericks stood again. "But you are taking Tolliver money."

"His company is paying my fee, yes." That would surprise them, to be so candid.

"That puts you on the same payroll as Alonzo Braden. Right, Mr. Hellinger?"

Nick gazed at him, causing Fredericks to shift his feet uneasily and glance around as if seeking support from his fellows in the trade. "I am not that familiar with how Mr. Tolliver keeps his books," Nick said calmly, "but I can tell you that it is not unknown for an employer to assist in the defense of a valued employee."

Another reporter, a grizzled man with a string tie, waved his pencil. "But a crusading journalist was murdered, Mr. Hellinger, and his anticrime series was coming pretty close to Clint Tolliver and some of his—"

"Paul Savage was a garbage disposal," Nick barked. This one was for Cara. "He was a conscienceless opportunist who would've pilloried his own mother for the sake of an extra Nielsen point." Tough for the print people to keep up on this, but great for TV. "In life, there's not one among you who wouldn't have crossed the street to avoid saying hello to your hallowed Paul Savage. In death, he's a hero fit for a Pulitzer. That's hypocrisy, gentlemen, is it not?" He let that sink in. Then he puffed up his chest and added in somber tones, "Because a member of the journalistic fraternity is murdered doesn't alter the face of justice!"

Several seconds passed before another reporter got up. It was a woman with teased hair and a big ribbon around her throat. "Mr. Hellinger, the police say they have no doubt at all that they have the right man, the murderer. Yet you say he is innocent. Can you give us anything at all to support your claim, against what the police tell us?"

"And against what you've been publishing?" He paused. "No, not here."

"But then all we have to go on is—"

"You're journalists, and I assume you're digging hard for the truth. Isn't that what all of you do? Well, there's a trial coming up soon. But you want to go ahead and try Alonzo Braden now in the press, ladies and gentlemen, be my guests. I'd like nothing better than a change of venue."

He turned from the podium, beckoned to Mrs. Braden, took her arm, and left the room, the babble following him.

"But Mr. Hellinger..."

"I wanted to ask..."

"Why won't you..."

They went quickly to the elevator, rode down, and hurried out through the lobby.

On the sidewalk, she said, "That was awful."

Nick smiled and tapped her arm. "In fact, it was a good beginning."

"They keep calling . . ."

"I've already ordered another phone for you, unlisted."

She leaned briefly against him. "Thanks. I just can't think of anything."

"You don't have to do anything. Just hold yourself together, and Julie."

"Lon is so tired."

"Yeah. But he's got plenty in reserve, believe me. He'll stand up to this."

"Such a nightmare. We're ruined, no matter what."

"Hey, what kind of talk is that?" He took her arms, looked into her eyes. "All that love you talked about between you."

"Yes." She nodded.

"That's a lot, honey, more than most people have to start with."

"I know."

"I can only ask you to be patient, Cara. Trust me, trust Lon. You are going to be very proud of your husband."

"There's something you're not telling me?"

"Hey, you want to know my plans for defense? You're worse than those hyenas in there!"

He was glad to elicit a chuckle from her, however dispirited.

A cab pulled up, Nick opened the door for her. "Don't worry about appearances, Cara. My experience around here is that nothing is as it seems. Get some sleep."

"I'll try." She settled herself in the cab. "You too. You look exhausted."

"My hang-dog look. Just for the press. Makes them think I'm earning my fee. Give Julie a hug for me."

He stopped by to see Braden briefly, fill him in

on the press conference.

"I wasn't too thrilled by Tolliver's legal establishment," Nick said. "Bunch of fuzz-heads—except for one young guy."

"Clay."

"Yeah. He seems healthily detached from the triumvirate."

"Doesn't sound like you left the press liking you too much."

"Better for us if they don't. You don't want them thinking I'm a good guy in a white hat, eh?"

"No, I guess not. Nothing new on the case, hunh? I mean nobody's come up with any clues to the murderer?"

"I'm afraid that's going to be pretty much up to me, from the looks of it."

"Well, the cops are the ones to do it, you know, and they think they've got their guy."

"Don't count me out. I may be just a humble city lawyer, but I can be down-home-country wily. I gotta run, got lots to do."

"Keep me posted, hunh?"

"Hey, who else do I have to talk to?"

The morning news was on TV with the sound turned low, and Nick bent down to buff his shoes with a towel, the telephone receiver held in the crook of his shoulder. "Hey, Dottie, a forty-six-yard field goal into the wind? Nobody should lose that way. I'm gonna start going to your church."

"They'd love you at AME Zion. Anyway, you can skip the sour grapes, counselor. I don't even know that much about football, and you owe me five bucks."

"We'll go double-or-nothing on Penn State next

Saturday. You ever get my car back from the tow heap?"

"Yup. And been enjoying it ever since. Rides like a dream."

"Yeah, you.... Listen, my ebony princess, as soon as your nail polish is dry, I've got some work for you."

"I'm all steno pad."

"Not all, but then that's a story for another time, and you probably hear it from all the boys. Listen, first I want you to shoot me everything you can dig up on the late, lamented Paul Savage. And I mean *everything*."

"Check."

"Second, call Joe Oliver at the Acme Detective Agency, tell him I need the name of a sharp PI in the Houston area, very much on the q.t. And somebody who can most definitely be trusted. Like with my life."

"Got it. Hold on a second, Judge Carroll would like to talk to you. You through with me?"

"For now, sugar, but not forever. Put him on."

The judge came on. "Nicholas? I expected to see you here this morning. I didn't find you, but I did receive a most agreeable surprise in the morning's mail. And not a moment too soon, I might add. Dottie's been saying we were running low on petty cash."

"You got a check from Tolliver."

"Yes, and my, haven't our fees climbed lately!"

"Don't deposit it. Hide it someplace until we know what we've got by the tail here."

"All right. But I assume from this that you decided to take the case after all."

"Yeah. Not for the money. Other things have come

up. You won't think less of me for it."

"Indeed? I have no way of knowing whether it's a good or a bad decision."

"*I* don't even know that."

"Curious . . ."

"Don't be. I didn't have much of an option, under the circumstances."

"About which you can't speak just now."

"Right."

"Ah, well . . . dear me, I'm late for court. My summation in the Forsythe matter."

"Make 'em weep, Judge."

"Oh, perhaps just a small tear in the corner of one eye of the jury foreman, if I should happen to strike a nerve . . ."

Nick hung up, chuckling. With a few of his well-chosen words of woe, the old rascal could reduce a roomful of sweathogs to lachrymosity in a medical disability suit like this.

Suddenly his attention was caught by the news on TV. Reporters were interviewing Anne Gronouski, the prosecutor on the Braden case. Even as he sprang to turn up the sound, he was struck by what a knockout she was, how she moved with athletic confidence and grace.

". . . just have nothing more I can say right now," she was telling them as they followed her to a car. "I'll leave the public pronouncements to counsel for the defense."

"You're confident of a conviction?" a newsman asked, sticking a microphone in her face.

"Naturally."

"And you did say you thought it would be a short trial?"

"I said I hoped it would. We are developing our

case quite properly and normally, and don't, from our part, expect a lengthy presentation of it." She started to enter the car, then couldn't resist, "If we can forgo Mr. Hellinger's widely celebrated penchant for theatrics, the trial should be short. Excuse me, gentlemen and ladies . . ."

She drove off. Nick smiled and clicked off the TV. Feisty broad. Young female prosecutors tended to be tougher than their male counterparts—sharper, better prepared, even more intelligent. Their road to the big time, of course, was more difficult. Those who accepted the challenge in the field of law tended to be the cream.

Eyes in the courtroom would follow her all the time. But Nick also knew that such good looks could work against her; there were those who sat on juries who resented such aggressive beauty, men and women alike.

You never knew, you just never knew. Be nice, though, if she were practicing in Philadelphia; lady worth getting to know.

"Ah, grief." Nick sighed as he took his jacket off the bed and pulled it on. "From the beauty to the beasts . . ."

Graebner's office was, unsurprisingly, all rich dark browns, thick carpet, leather chairs and sofa, leather-topped desk, heavy funereal drapes. Graebner needed more sun and less booze, judging from his complexion.

The senior partner had gathered Wilkes and Cassellman, along with junior associate Andy Clay, in the spacious room, and when everyone was comfortably seated, coffee served by his secretary, Graebner leaned across his desk and folded his ruddy hands.

"Our instructions from Mr. Tolliver are quite simple, gentlemen." His voice sounded like he needed to clear his throat. "We are to win Mr. Braden's freedom at any cost. Since the district attorney will not accept our proposals for a deal . . ."

Nick had not been aware of any attempts to cop a plea.

". . . we're left with limited options. Temporary insanity, self-defense—"

"Or we can believe his story," Clay interrupted, "that someone else killed Paul Savage just before he got there."

Now Graebner cleared his throat and fidgeted with his hands. He tilted his head up and looked at Clay down his nose. "Really, Andrew, your naïveté is a constant astonishment to me."

Clay flushed. "Naiveté? Because I suggest that our client may be innocent?"

The kid didn't back off quickly. Nick watched them both.

"Had there been an intruder," Graebner went on with the tried patience of a prep-school master and such condescension, "as the defendant alleges, why was nothing stolen?"

Nick wondered at the use of "defendant" as if the man were not their client. Who were these monkeys?

"And if not an intruder, then who? Someone else who was afraid of what Savage might say on his broadcast? Oh, yes, Braden was afraid, he's said as much. Of what? We are left to guess. But as to someone else in a similar predicament, who might that be? Someone we know? It should be obvious even to you that were we to pursue that line, we'd be right back in the same disturbing circumstance. Ah, Andrew, I'm not saying Mr. Braden is guilty, I am describing how it looks, how it will look to a jury. And we have our job to do."

"Which is," Clay said bitterly, "to protect Clinton Tolliver and his organization at any cost."

Wilkes and Cassellman stiffened in their chairs. Graebner's face turned redder.

"Yes, my young man, as you so impertinently put it! But whatever the cost to Mr. Tolliver, that is none of your concern. Nor do we need to be distracted by your blue-sky theories. We have more than enough difficulty in dealing with simple reality here!"

"I'm also interested in justice," Andy shot back.

"You are also excused. I'll talk to you later, Andrew."

Andy headed for the door. "Like hell you will." He slammed the door behind him.

Nick had risen also.

Graebner turned his attention to him. "Please accept my apologies, Mr. Hellinger, and sit down. We'll all have to forgive the boy's impetuousness and intemperance."

Nick remained standing. "I don't have to forgive him. I think he's right. I also happen to think Lon Braden is innocent."

"Well, we all suppose so, but that's not the real issue here."

"Oh no? Well, pardon me. Perhaps I've been misled by my limited education and meager experience."

"Please, Mr. Hellinger. Keep in mind that we have not been employed by Mr. Braden, but by—"

"Gentlemen,"—Nick picked up his hat—"if you want to protect your meal ticket, that's your lookout. Me, I have only one obligation—to defend my client."

"You've perhaps forgotten that your fee comes from—"

"I've forgotten nothing, Graebner. Including what I was paid to do. I'm going to defend Lon Braden. And if Mr. Tolliver gets muddied up in the process, that's his tough luck. He made the deal, left the rest up to me."

"Beg your pardon, Mr. Hellinger, he left it up to *us*, including you."

"As of now, friend, one of us is off the case."

"Now just a minute." Graebner half rose from his chair. "You can't just decide—"

"I've already been paid. So I've got a job to do. Ta-ta."

Once in the hallway, Nick permitted himself a small, quick chuckle. A little harsh, he thought, but on the whole, well done, Hellinger; the decks were clear.

Graebner had a large corner office. What Nick was looking for now, he suspected, was a very small interior one, away from the windows. He went along the hallway glancing into each office.

Halfway down the hall, he found it. Not much more than a cubbyhole. A desk, a chair, a filing cabinet. A few moments before there had been a couple of pictures on the wall. But Andy Clay had just now taken them down and was packing them into a carton.

He was muttering to himself. He slammed the chair against the desk. He ripped open a file drawer, almost toppling the cabinet.

Nick stood in the doorway, watching with some amusement—not that he didn't sympathize, but Andy was such a gritty young lawyer, he would do just fine.

Andy didn't see him for a couple of minutes. Finally Nick spoke.

"Some stuff nobody ever told you, hunh?"

"What?" Andy spun, ready for a confrontation. He quickly unclenched his hands. "Oh. Told me what, Mr. Hellinger?"

"That children should be seen but not heard."

"I'm not a kid!"

"Easy, easy." Nick held up a hand as if to protect his face. "I didn't say, or even mean to imply, that you were. But you don't have the hashmarks yet to get salty with your elders."

"Yeah, well, they won't have this child to kick around anymore." He resumed packing, taking out files and dumping them into a box.

"Walking out, hunh, just like that?"

"Damn right. I may be young, but I'm a goddamned lawyer! I passed the same bar they did. If this is Graebner, Wilkes, and Casselman's idea of law, they know where they can stick it!"

"The law's not cut and dried, Andrew, not black and white."

"The *idea* of law is. Don't give me the old lecture about flexibility."

"And just what might be your idea of law, young Master Clay?"

"To give every client," he responded quickly, punctuating each phrase with the dropping of a folder into the box, "regardless of social background or economic status, the kind of legal representation to which he's constitutionally entitled."

"Mmm." Nick cocked his head. "Saintly sentiments."

"I didn't dream them up."

"I didn't imagine so. Quite old and trite and familiar."

"They ought to be familiar. They were in the commencement address you gave to my graduating class at Virginia Law."

Nick couldn't help laughing.

"What's so funny?" Andy frowned.

"That was old and trite even then. But, good speech, good school. I'm glad you went there. You got a good foundation. You'll work out just fine."

"What do you mean?"

Graebner came up behind Nick and cleared his throat. Nick turned out of the room to face him.

"Mr. Hellinger—Nick—excuse me. I want to apologize."

"Oh?"

"I believe we both said things, in the heat of debate, that we shouldn't have said."

"Not me."

"Oh, I don't mean about the minor disagreements." He fluttered his hands as if chasing bugs. "Those things happen all the time. I mean the business about, well, one of us being off the case."

"I know what you mean. I said what I meant."

"Well now"—Graebner rubbed his mouth thoughtfully—"we both know you can't defend Braden on your own."

"Believe it or not, I've defended clients on my own before, without my hand even being held."

"That's not what I mean."

"You have trouble saying what you mean."

"What I mean is you must have an attorney of record, licensed to practice in the state of Texas!" He was triumphant.

Nick grinned. "Oh, but I do have one, Mr. Graebner."

"What? Who?"

"Him." Nick jabbed a thumb toward Andy Clay.

Graebner took a stumbling step backward. Air seemed to leave him as from a balloon—he seemed actually to get smaller. Then he turned and scurried off down the hall, shaking his head.

Andy leaned heavily against the file cabinet, his mouth open.

Nick smiled. "Come on, finish packing, let's go." And he added, under his breath, "Well done, Hellinger."

CHAPTER 6

"I AM not a nice guy, Mr. Tolliver," Nick said into the telephone, "when I'm defending a client charged with murder." His free arm cradled his head on the pillow. He looked over his crossed bare feet at the silent TV.

"Attorney Graebner has been with me a long time," Tolliver drawled, "a faithful servant, dedicated."

"If he's like a son to you, then that puts him in a flat-footed tie with Lon Braden. But Braden's ass is in a sling, and I don't give a damn about Graebner. You hired me to get your man off, you can discharge me. But I can't work with your faithful Attorney Graebner. I've made my choice, you can make yours."

Tolliver was speaking carefully, not angrily, feeling Nick out. "It makes me quite nervous that this would all happen the day before the bind-over hearing. Would it, unh, be your intention to follow Mr. Graebner's strategy for the hearing?"

"What strategy? There's no strategy here. They've got him cold on probable cause. I'm not even going to argue it."

Tolliver paused. "You're just going to let it go to trial?"

"Look, they arrested Braden at the scene—trying to flee the scene, in fact. They have no other suspect. What's to argue? You'd just get everybody all cranked up, the result would be the same. Plus, I'm not about to spill anything I want to use at trial."

"You have something, then?"

"You think I've been sitting on my ass?"

"Can you give me an idea of what—"

"No."

"You mean not over the phone?"

"I mean no. You'll have to let me do it my way. The farther you stay away from all this the better. And I have to ask you to stay away from Braden too, no contact at all. Let it be just him and me and his family."

"You underestimate me, Nick. You think I would be stupid enough to visit him in jail or come to court? With how they're trying to use our relationship against him?"

"I mean when he's out."

"You're going to get him out?"

"I'm going to try for bail. And the best way for that is to make it look like there's just him and me and his wife and daughter. The hearing judge might be merciful to Mr. Homebody under the wing of his responsible attorney."

Tolliver hesitated. "I see."

"I sincerely hope so. I gotta get ready for court, Mr. Tolliver."

"Clint."

"Yeah."

The hearing room was packed with spectators, a good many of them members of the press. There was an air of heavy anticipation for the first courtroom appearance of Nick Hellinger. There had been stories in the papers about Nick's more famous cases, his dramatic defenses. Cara Braden was not present, her husband had asked her not to come, not to this part of it.

Anne Gronouski was presenting her case to show "probable cause" sufficient to have the case bound over to the Grand Jury for indictment of the defendant. She was dressed primly, her hair tied back with a ribbon. No matter how she dressed, she looked entirely feminine, beautiful. But her method and demeanor were entirely professional.

On the stand was the first police officer to arrive on the scene, the one who caught Braden in Paul Savage's backyard.

"Describe that for the court," Anne said, "if you please."

"We both got out of the car, me and my partner. He went to the front, I went around to the back. I saw this guy—"

"We have established that it was night. Would you describe the weather conditions?"

"Oh, yeah. It was clear, there was a moon, some

moonlight. Enough to see outlines of things."

"Go on."

"Okay. I saw this guy running away—"

"Running away?"

"I mean, away from the house, in the direction opposite the house. I identified myself as a police officer and ordered him to stop."

"And did he stop?"

"Yes, ma'am. He fell. I put my flashlight on him. Then my partner come around, and I saw the doors was open in the back, so I told him he better check inside."

"And did he do so?"

"He did, yes, ma'am. And when he come out, he said we got a dead body in there. So I put this man under arrest."

"Did he resist in any way?"

"No, ma'am. I had my flashlight and gun on him, and my partner put the cuffs on him. He just come along and we took him in."

Anne nodded and thought for a moment. "The man you apprehended, do you see him in this courtroom?"

"Yes, ma'am. That's him over there." He pointed to Braden, who was sitting glumly between Nick and Andy Clay.

"Indicating the suspect, Alonzo Braden. No further questions, Your Honor."

The judge looked over the tops of his bifocals. "Mr. Hellinger?"

An expectant rustle went through the courtroom as people shifted to the fronts of the wooden benches.

"No questions." Nick didn't rise from his table.

"Very well. Mr. Hellinger, do you wish to call any witnesses at this time?"

"No, Your Honor."

A murmur of disappointment rumbled through the crowd. The judge quieted them with a stern look over his glasses.

Then he said, "Very well. The defendant will rise." Braden stood. "I find that sufficient evidence has been presented at this hearing and order that the defendant be bound over to the Grand Jury for a determination."

He was about to rap his gavel when Nick got to his feet.

"Your Honor?"

"Mr. Hellinger?"

"If I might approach the Bench—with the prosecution, of course."

The judge motioned them forward.

Nick spoke softly. "I'd like to ask that bail be set in this case, Your Honor."

"Bail!" Anne glared at him. "This is murder, Mr. Hellinger."

"If I may?" Nick raised his eyebrows to her, then addressed the judge. "Your Honor, despite the seriousness of the charge, no evidence has been shown to suggest motive or premeditation. And as the prosecution may have noticed, I have made no attempt to delay the case or confuse the issue. I would like to point out that Mr. Braden is a family man, with a small daughter. They are long-standing members of the community. Mr. Braden has never so much as received a parking ticket. And beyond that, I would offer myself as evidence of good faith in this case. I am here from Philadelphia precisely because of the seriousness of the charge, and the fact that I firmly believe my client to be innocent. Moreover, the intent of my presence is that the matter be brought to trial as soon as possible, so that my client may be cleared and may resume his normal life, right here. I believe my record will show that I have an unblemished reputation for producing my clients for trial. Mr. Braden has already spent several days in jail. His family needs him. I will personally take full responsibility for his appearance in court on the appointed date, should the Grand Jury return an indictment. I ask for the sympathy of the court—and the prosecution."

"Miss Gronouski?"

"A moving speech, Your Honor. I have no inclination to be unduly harsh in my insistence—"

"You have a daughter yourself," Nick said gently, "do you not?"

"That's hardly the issue!"

"She's right, counselor," the judge said. "Proceed."

Anne licked her lips. "I am aware of Mr. Hellinger's reputation. And I am aware that the purpose of bail is solely to guarantee the defendant's appearance for trial, not a punishment in itself. So, all right. But I think that bail should be high enough to add further inducement for the defendant to remain in this jurisdiction and to appear."

"Thank you, Miss Gronouski." Nick bowed slightly.

She didn't look at him.

"All right." The judge waved them away. They went back to their tables. The judge adopted a most serious look. "I order that bail in this case be set for one hundred thousand dollars," he announced.

"Thank you, Your Honor," Nick said, bowing to the bench.

Anne slammed her attaché case shut.

Braden smiled with relief. Andy Clay looked awed.

Court was adjourned, the spectators stood while the judge left the room.

Then Nick said, "Okay, Lon, you're out—just as soon as I arrange for some pocket money to be transferred from my bank to the court. Now all we gotta do is beat a murder rap."

Braden flinched.

"Sorry, bad joke. Anyway, go join the officers. I'll make arrangements and pick you up. Give me a few minutes. Andy, out in the hall."

"Hunh?"

"With me. Come on."

They hurried out, Andy right on Nick's heels.

"Get your notebook ready," Nick said over his shoulder.

Andy took out a pocket-size memo pad. As soon as they were in the corridor, Nick turned to him.

"Write." Andy readied his pen.

"Graebner dismissed the intruder theory on the basis that nothing was taken from Savage's study. Do we know that for a fact?"

"I don't know if—"

"Write it down. I want photos of the crime scene, transcripts of Detective Donovan's case notes, reports, everything. They give you any static, tell 'em we'll have a court order in five minutes. Am I going too fast for you?"

Andy scribbled furiously. "I minored in shorthand." He glanced up. "But I don't make coffee."

"Clever. Now, contact what's-her-name—Savage's assistant."

"Laura Weire."

"Yeah. Find out who else besides our client was due for a hatchet job."

"From *her?*" Andy shook his head. "The way she felt about her boss? No way we'll get cooperation from that lady!"

"Ah, Andy." Nick patted his shoulder heavily. "That kind of talk does not make me a happy man. There is never *no* way. We are an optimistic duo, are we not?" He gave Andy's shoulder a severe squeeze, making Andy wince. "Hellinger's Law: There is no such thing as an uncommunicative source—there are only unresourceful lawyers."

Andy made a note. "I'll try."

"Not try, son . . ."

"I'll do it."

"Yeah." He handed him a hotel key. "I've rented a suite on the top floor. Have them clear out the tourist furniture, put in three desks, typewriters, phones, copying machine. And get a coffee machine we can run ourselves. That'll be our office. Any questions? Good."

Before Andy could reply, Nick moved off through the milling crowd.

Anne Gronouski was near the elevators talking with a male assistant.

"Miss Gronouski."

She looked up, frowned.

"That was a nifty presentation, counselor." Nick smiled graciously. "Not an ounce of fat on it. My compliments." He dipped his head.

Her smile was frigid. "My, my, praise from Caesar?" She dismissed the assistant with a wave of the hand and watched him walk away. Then she turned to Nick and restored the icy smile. "Should I blush, curtsy, demurely avert my eyes?"

"Not those eyes, my dear. They should never be averted. They are worth a prize."

She dropped her smile, looked stony.

"But that aside, I was just telling you the truth. You're smooth and efficient. I'm not just being Mr.

Nice Guy. It pays to notice things like that. More cases have been lost through underestimating one's opponent than by intransigent jurisprudence."

"Indeed? A quote for the ages. I must try and remember who said it." She put a finger to her cheek and knitted her brows. "Oliver Wendell Holmes?"

"Nicholas Metaxis Hellinger." He bowed. "And don't forget it."

"How could I? You're the one and only. Float like a butterfly, sting like a bee."

"Muhammad Ali, maybe, but actually I don't float."

"I've read your press clippings, Mr. Hellinger."

"Ah."

"I was even required to study some of your more notorious litigations at law school."

"Notorious?"

"Notable, if you prefer. In any event, you're not news to me. Rest assured, I shall not underestimate my opponent."

She was a real match, this lady. Never missed a beat. Among her nice physical lines was that of her jaw, which was firm. "So you've got my number, hunh?"

She smiled slowly. "That, Mr. Hellinger, would be underestimating you."

"Yeah. The big Philadelphia shyster come to God's country—deep in the heart of it—to play mouthpiece for the mob, and in the process slicker you out of a twenty-four-karat conviction. That would sting some, wouldn't it? That would be a big setback for an ambitious young prosecutor who most certainly wishes to put herself in line for her boss's job."

She stared at him.

"I also read press clippings, Mrs. Gronouski."

"Miss."

"Sorry."

"You knew that. I'm sure the clippings must have called me a divorcée, they usually do."

"Yeah. Actually, I'm tired of being nasty."

"Good, so am I."

Nick brightened. "Okay, so we're both ambitious lawyers on the make. Kin under the skin. We both have to eat, right? How about lunch?"

"I don't eat lunch." She was wary, didn't smile, but the iciness was gone.

"Dinner, then? I've found this dynamite little place, they serve a terrific crab-and-mushroom salad—"

"Turley's. It's a tourist trap."

"Beautiful! Let's pretend we're from out of town."

"A bit unorthodox, don't you think? The two of us?"

"I stopped being orthodox when I lost my first honest defense."

She chuckled, raised one eyebrow. "What is this mysterious power you supposedly have over women?"

"Where'd you read that? Same place you got the butterfly and the bee?"

"I sniffed it. I can also sniff a snow job. I am not going to talk about this case."

"Ah, Miss Prosecutor, take another deep breath. I promise"—he held up his right hand—"we will not talk shop."

"I won't forget that either."

"Later, then." He tapped her arm and started away. "I got a client to bail out."

"I know, I know." Nick reached over to the passenger

side to tap Lon Braden's cheek. "Save it for the acquittal."

"But I just can't believe it. I never expected to get out like this."

"It isn't a miracle. I never said anything because I wasn't sure it would work myself."

"Is it a good sign, Nick, that I got out on bail?"

"Every morning we wake up is a good sign."

"I've been trying to remember stuff that might help in the defense. I can't think of anything."

"Your job is Tolliver. Spend your time remembering things you'll need for that. My job is you. I switch into high gear now. I'll keep you posted."

They pulled over in front of Braden's house. Immediately the house door opened and Cara and Julie trotted down the steps.

Braden slid out the passenger side. "You're coming in, aren't you?"

"No, not now. Enjoy yourselves. And don't talk to anybody but me. Not even Tolliver. I think Rossetti knows enough to stay away. Beat it, they're waiting."

Braden fell into an embrace with his wife. Julie hugged his legs from behind. They started for the house. Julie looked back.

Nick slipped the lucky shamrock out of his pocket, flipped it, then held it up for her to see. He blew her a kiss, she returned it and ran to join her parents as they went in the door.

Nick parked a block away from the restaurant and went into a phone booth. Dottie had passed on the name, then done a little further checking on her own, just to be sure. She graded the guy an "A."

"Manolo Shelldrake?"

"Who's calling?"

"Nicholas Hellinger."

"It's me, Mr. Hellinger. When you want to meet?"

"I don't. Too much attention on me down here, Shelldrake. My information is that you can be trusted, I'll have to go with that. You'll be working with my associate, a young lawyer named Andy Clay. He'll brief you. But I can tell you right off, we don't have much to go on."

"I don't usually get called in on cases that are wrapped up, Mr. Hellinger."

"It'll be tricky. You'll have to work the crime scene some."

"Never found a place yet I couldn't get into and out of, and nobody ever saw my name in the papers."

"Stay by the phone."

Good. Shelldrake was cool and confident. If he was as good a private investigator as Joe Oliver at Acme said he was, they had a shot at finding something. Nick hoped there was something to find.

The restaurant featured fake Tiffany lamps and waitresses dressed in pioneer garb. They both had the crab-and-mushroom salad. Nick asked Anne about herself.

She picked at her salad. "Married young—my daughter's sixteen. My husband ran a construction business, he put me through law school. He was always opposed to me going to school. He wanted me home with Bonnie. He also didn't want me being a lawyer. Maybe it was because the construction business was so filled with payoffs and so forth. Anyway, you can see we weren't particularly well attuned to each other."

"How long did you stick it out?"

"Ten long years. He was a handsome guy, big strong galoot. One day he bought another construction business in Oklahoma City. Another day he picked up and moved there. Another day not long after that, I got a divorce in Reno."

"Hmm. Why law?"

"I knew I was going to need a career, figured I'd be on my own some day. I figured you could do anything with a law degree, maybe even go into politics. I tend to be meticulous, logical. I got a job with a private firm. My idea was to defend the innocent. But they treated me like a flunky there, and I got chased around desks a lot. Plus the firm was doing a lot of very successful business defending white-collar thieves against weak prosecutions. So I switched sides. That's where you've found me."

Their plates were cleared, brandy served. They touched snifters in salute.

Anne swirled the brandy in the belly of her glass, warming it against her palm, then she sipped. "Hmm, wonderful."

"Aged in oak. It's potent."

"That why you ordered it?"

"Not necessarily. I don't want your mind fuzzed up. Among your other obvious qualities, I appreciate your mind."

"Very charming." She smiled.

"True."

"Thank you." She examined her fingernails. "Mind if I ask you a question?"

"Depends."

"Why *did* you take this case? I mean, it's been on my mind, I've been curious about it. I *have* read your press clippings, you see, and I feel that I know quite a bit about your work and your style. I'm convinced that you believe Braden is innocent of the murder, but what about the rest of it?"

"That's two questions."

"Okay, I assume you took the case because you believe he's innocent. But there's still the rest of it."

"He's not on trial for what you call 'the rest of it.'"

"I'm not sure it's separable. Putting aside all the legal niceties, Braden belongs in prison—if not for murder, for collusion with that bunch of—"

"Irrelevant and immaterial." Nick leaned across the table. "Appealing and righteous as you are, you try convicting my client for the company he keeps, lady, and I'll eat you alive."

"I don't intend to be stupid. I said I was just curious."

"We made a pact, remember? No shoptalk." He smiled and sipped his brandy.

"Okay."

"So I know about your marriage. You never married again. Am I being nosy to ask why not?"

"No, it's okay. Too much career, too little home life, you know. I don't even spend the time now I should with my daughter."

"That all?"

Her lips twitched in a slight smile. "Maybe I lost a little faith in the whole business, from the first time around. You?"

"Ah, me. I came close three times. I was serious, too."

"Three times."

"Yeah. Missed by an inch every time."

"You get discouraged either easily or early."

"Despite what you may infer from my reputation, I'm really a very cautious man."

"But that's exactly what I deduced. You take chances when necessary, to be sure. But otherwise you leave nothing to chance. Very thorough, you are. I don't mistake theatrics for substance."

"Despite what I may see on TV."

"Yes." She laughed.

"Good for you. But don't spread it around. There are people who think I'm just crazy and lucky."

"Unlucky in love, lucky in law."

"Good line."

"Well, I guess the law *has* been good to us. We're both doing okay, pretty much what we want to do."

"Pretty much."

"Did you always want to practice law?"

"Oh, my." Nick rolled his eyes up. "Time for another brandy." He ordered a round.

"So tell me."

"Naw, I bloomed late. My father . . . died when I was a teenager . . ."

"Oh, I'm sorry. Can I ask—"

"Don't. I don't talk about it. Anyway, he wanted me to be a doctor. I wanted to be a cop."

"A cop. That's hard to imagine."

"Don't kid yourself, I was never a big fan of the bad guys—still not. So I did my stint as an MP with the Provost Marshal's office in Seoul, in Korea. Watched a lot of court-martials, saw the legal system in action—at least the GI version of it. Well, once I saw a kid, hardly old enough to shave, get twenty years in Leavenworth for a crime I never thought he committed. His defense counsel was a lieutenant still wet behind the ears, so green he couldn't draw up a will, let along defend a guy in a trumped-up sodomy case. And the prosecutor didn't give a damn who he convicted just so he convicted somebody. After the defendant heard the sentence, he strung himself up by his shirt in the guardhouse."

"Wow. And you were pretty sure he was innocent."

"Yeah, I was sure. I knew the kid. I binged for a couple of days. Then I went out and found the guy who set him up. I managed to wheedle a confession out of him, by breaking his jaw and a couple of ribs. Too late for the poor innocent bastard who hung himself."

"So you decided to be a defense attorney."

"Not directly. I had spent some time in the Police Academy before Korea. I wanted the law, yes, but I still had a lot of cop in me. And I figured the prosecutor had a responsibility to go after the right guy. I wanted the bad guys put away. So when the Army let me loose, I went to law school. Then eventually the U.S. Attorney's office."

"Somewhere along the line you switched sides."

"You could say that. I got this funny idea that justice is on both sides of the courtroom aisle. But yeah, I switched. What the hell, I figured that both sides deserved a chance to employ my superior skills."

"Hmm. It's odd, thinking . . ."

"Thinking what?"

"Well, I guess we're both sitting here thinking that the other is on the wrong side in this case."

"All I'm thinking is, you're on the opposite side of the table. And the view from this side is pleasant."

She chuckled. "I should be getting home. Got a big case I should be preparing for—you too."

Nick signaled for the check.

"We'll split it." She reached for her purse.

"Nonsense."

"Chauvinist?"

"Irrelevant and immaterial and who the hell knows? What's relevant is I got plenty of room on my expense account."

"I'm not sure I like the idea of, of . . ."

"Of my employer paying for your dinner? Don't worry, lady. Whatever else you may think of my ethics, I got no problem at all soaking my employer for every penny I can on this particular case."

She laughed. "Okay."

In the car, he asked her if she still liked Houston, after all these years.

"Sure. It's busy and booming. It's got all the problems of the biggest cities, and more than enough of what you call the bad guys dealing in dope and prostitution and all the rackets."

"Good place to make your reputation."

"Yup."

"And how about the rest of it?"

"To paraphrase you, since you have just paraphrased me . . ."

"Whoo, you don't forget a word."

". . . I'm not on trial here for the rest of it. It's hot, it's humid, it's not L.A. or New York, but it's home."

"But you don't want to be here forever."

"You guessed right. I'd like to see another part of the country. But I'll stay here long enough for my daughter to grow up and get on her own. Then we'll see. By then, I might feel like backing out of the rat race. Maybe I'll buy a farm in Vermont."

"Not much money in Vermont."

"So, I'll milk cows and make a small living doing occasional real-estate closings. Inside this tough-minded prosecutor, Mr. Hellinger, there is a small-town country girl trying to get out."

"And inside this tough-minded Philadelphia shyster, Miss Gronouski, is a guy who hopes you get your wish."

"Thank you, Nick."

"My pleasure, Anne." He tapped her hand. She gripped his briefly.

She lived in a modest ranch-style house in a well-kept neighborhood of similar houses. Nick pulled into the driveway and followed her to the front door. The heavy beat of rock music came from inside.

"Can I offer you a nightcap?"

"Unorthodox."

"Aren't we, though?"

In the foyer, he helped her off with her light coat. The music boomed from the rear of the house.

Anne grimaced. "My daughter's into self-inflicted deafness." She called back, "Bonnie? Honey, I'm home!"

No response. She shrugged. She led him into the living room and indicated the bar at the far end. "Why don't you build us something appropriate over ice? I'll see if I can get the disco under control. Be back in a jiff."

Her step was lighter than before, kittenish. It was as enjoyable watching her walk away as facing her.

Abruptly the music went off. Nick heard Anne shout, "Bonnie!" Then something crashed.

For a second Nick wondered whether it was any of his business. Then he hurried in the direction of the noise.

"Randy!" he heard Anne shout.

He came to the door of what once might have been a playroom for a little girl. The only light was the shaft of it that came from the hall outside the door where he was standing.

A teenage boy was wrestling with the knob of the back door, trying to button his shirt at the same time. Bonnie, her blouse open, was lying back on the sofa, propped up on her elbows. Between the sofa and the back door, the turntable lay in pieces on the floor, apparently knocked over by the boy in his flight.

Finally Randy worked the door open and fled into the night.

Anne had been standing as if paralyzed. Now she reached back and flicked on the light switch.

Bonnie blinked. She was pretty, pale, her eyes unfocused. Her voice was thick and slurred. "D'you suppose it's true that Wonder Woman is on the pill?"

Anne knelt beside the sofa, then her eyes fell on an open plastic pill bottle of white powder at her feet. She snatched it up. "What is this? Bonnie, baby, *what?*"

Bonnie giggled. Anne grabbed her shoulders, shook her.

"You've got to tell me what you've taken!"

"Just dust, Mommy." She giggled. "Dust for your li'l angel."

"Angel dust! Oh, my God, no!"

Bonnie rolled over and waggled a finger at Nick. "Look, it's Daddy Warbucks! Hi, there."

Anne was on her feet, a hand at the side of her head. She stared at the bottle, at Bonnie. "No . . . goddamn it, no . . ."

"Wow," Bonnie said, still looking dully at Nick, "is she ever in a groushy mood." Her words were slurred.

Anne spun toward Nick. "What are you doing here?"

"I heard you shout, heard noise, I—"

"Get the hell out of here!"

Nick eyed her for a second, blinked slowly, then nodded and withdrew.

Anne followed, shutting the door behind her. "Sorry," she muttered, "sorry . . . for yelling . . ." She clenched the pill bottle in her hand.

"Take it easy." He tried to console her by putting an arm around her. She slid away. "I'm not the enemy, Anne. I just happened to be here. I want to—"

"Please leave." She was controlling her voice—no small effort.

"Okay, okay, I won't be in your way. But maybe we could talk for a minute. This is not a bottle of Ripple wine those kids were fooling with in there. This is—"

"I know what it is! I know what I'm dealing with!"

"You won't let me help?"

"You bought me dinner, Hellinger! That doesn't entitle you to a slice of my private life!" She couldn't look at him. She was near cracking. She said more softly, "Please."

"Yeah. Okay."

As he headed for the front door, he heard Bonnie's voice, weak and choked, call from behind the closed playroom door, "Mommy? Can I have a glass of milk?"

He let himself out, closed the door, and stood on the front steps, his eyes closed.

"Christ," he mumbled. "Oh, Christ, Anne, the bastards won't leave anybody alone."

Driving to his hotel, he could think only of how all the evil shit in the world always trickled down to the kids. Somehow, the kids always got hurt. How he loved kids. How afraid he was for them. Kids whose fathers got shot in the neck; kids whose fathers tried to help society and got charged with murder; kids who could buy drugs on the street because somebody in Marseille or Colombia or Miami or the Bronx or Houston was getting rich off it.

Could he ever dare to have kids? In a world like this? Where there were guys like Clint Tolliver dipping their fingers into any vicious business that turned a profit, regardless of destroying families, hurting kids?

All he could do was work, and he could hope that overall he was helping society. But there was so pitifully little he could do. He could beat the unfair rap on Braden, return him to his family, hope he would be safe. And that would be his contribution to nailing that bastard Tolliver.

But he couldn't help so worthy a lonely, hardworking, justice-seeking soul like Anne Gronouski when it really counted.

No, big-shot attorney Nicholas Hellinger, he thought, you are not so potent after all.

CHAPTER 7

IN THE early morning, the park was nearly deserted except for a few joggers. Most of them were in shorts and T-shirts. One, Nick, was in a blue nylon warm-up suit and a Phillies cap. It was unusually cool, but Nick always dressed that way—always meaning whenever he got around to jogging, which was more often than not when he had a special amount of tension to steam off. He had bought a pair of New Balance running shoes—recommended by the lean kid at the running shop—and they were already giving him blisters. Nick was not fat, but he could feel the excess flab he did have jiggle over the waistband. He was breathing hard after a half-mile. Other joggers passed him, gliding along like they could run forever. One guy had to be sixty years old. It was depressing.

He heard a bell jingle behind him, saw Andy catching up on a bicycle, and slowed to a walk.

Andy pulled alongside. In the basket on the handlebars were a couple of large envelopes and a paper bag.

Nick swung his arms and took deep, gasping breaths.

"Didn't know you were a jogger," Andy said.

"They say it's . . . good for your . . . sex life."

"Oh, yeah?"

"You should've been here earlier."

"Oh? I missed something?"

"No, but I could've stopped earlier. You got something?"

"Yes and no. We need to talk. You eat yet?"

"Never eat before you run, kid."

"Good. I brought breakfast."

They wandered over to a picnic table in the middle of the park, Andy wheeling his bike. They sat opposite each other. Nick wiped the sweat off his forehead with his hand. His heart was beating hard—he hoped it would understand how healthful this was.

Andy handed him a taco wrapped in wax paper.

"This time of morning?" Nick winced.

"You said you liked them."

"Yeah, well—"

"Wake you up." He poured coffee from a thermos into styrofoam cups.

"Yeah, like a punch to the solar plexus. Okay, what've you got?"

Andy shoved the manila envelopes across the table to him. "Savage worked from notes. There never was a prepared script. He was always talking security, so he kept it in his head. He just went on the air and winged it. Up to showtime, according to his assistant, that girl Laura, even she didn't know what bombshells he intended to unload."

Nick sat slumped, waiting to get his breath. "So I don't suppose she was helpful about his sources."

"Nope, she didn't know much. Her boss played it so close to the vest. She said she'd been with him a year before he broke down and gave her his unlisted phone number."

"A real fountain of information, this babe. Unless she plays it close to the vest too."

Andy straightened. "She wasn't holding back on me, if that's what you're suggesting."

"Oh, really? You seemed to be pretty sure she wouldn't cooperate. What makes you so sure she wasn't playing cozy?"

"The lady bowls. I've got the thumb to prove it." He held up the bandaged right digit. "We musta bowled a hundred lines."

"So, what do you want from me, a Purple Heart? Bowling ain't talking."

"She drinks beer. We had fun. She loosened up. She . . . well, she liked me. I could tell she was being honest. It was like she really wished she *had* known more about what was going on. She wanted to be part of the operation, wanted to be more on the inside. She wanted to be an investigator, but she kind of got locked into being his go-for at the station. In any case, I believe her."

Nick sipped his coffee, musing. "He worked from notes, she said."

"Right."

"Based on what?"

"She didn't say."

"He must've kept files of some kind."

"I don't know where." Andy shook his head. "Not at his office, that's for sure. And not at his home either."

"How you know that?"

"That private detective you hired, Shelldrake? He checked the place out, top to bottom."

"You're sure?"

"The guy seems very straight to me, Nick, very thorough. He didn't want to tell me how he got in, but he did tell me about his search, all the details and so forth of where he looked. He was there, all right. Nothing but innocuous letters, books..."

"Then he bungled it. They *have* to be there."

"But if he has files, they could be *anywhere*, Nick."

"No, I don't think so. I think he would want them right with him all the time, right at his fingertips. Damn!" He chomped down on a big bite of taco. Suddenly his eyes bulged, he gasped, reached for the coffee, and took a swig. "What the hell *is* this?"

"Little hot for you? I had 'em spice it up good, thought you liked 'em hot."

"Hot ain't the word for this, kid. At this hour of the morning, it's all I can do to get through a prune danish."

"Sorry." Andy poured more coffee.

"These photos of the crime scene?" Nick opened one of the envelopes.

"Yeah. About a dozen eight-by-tens. I studied them pretty carefully, couldn't find anything new."

The photos were taken from various angles by a camera with a flash attachment. Several showed the corpse lying on the floor. Others, taken after the body's removal, showed a taped outline where the body had been. The poker—the murder weapon—was on the floor, so was Savage's .32 automatic. From some angles, the tape recorder was visible. In one, the lower legs of three men were included, two pairs clearly belonging to uniformed cops, one somebody in street clothes. The pants and shoes were blotched with water marks.

"Braden," Nick mumbled.

"Hunh?"

"Nothing. Just that this is Braden's feet here, with the cops, sloppy with water from the damn rainbirds in the backyard, damned sprinklers he tripped over."

"So?"

"He didn't tell me they took him back inside. I don't like him forgetting details like that, even if they aren't important." Nick shuffled through more pictures. Then he paused, returned to a picture he had passed. He raised his eyebrows, and slid the picture over to Andy. "Here. Tell me what you see."

"The tape recorder."

"What about it? Come on, man, *details!*"

"Nothing about it. There's nothing on it. Just the empty—"

"Right! Nothing on it. Not even a *take-up reel.*"

"Yeah?" Andy stared hard at the photo.

"But there, on the floor"—Nick jabbed at the section of the photo with his index finger—"there's an empty carton lying there."

"Oh, yeah."

"What does that suggest to you, Andrew?"

"A tape. Not in the box. Not on the machine . . ."

"Gone! As in somebody took!"

Andy looked quizzical. "You think that was involved in the killing? A tape?"

"It's a start, isn't it? Think about it. Somebody there before Braden, a tape was being played. For some reason there was no time to rewind it. Maybe because Braden was at the door?" He leaned over and narrowed his eyes at Andy.

"I see, possibility..."

"A theory, hunh? Follow it another step. The guy wanted the tape, had to have it. All of a sudden he became a murderer. He grabbed both reels of it and split. But"—Nick held up a finger—"he left the machine running. Suppose that was the humming sound that Braden heard?"

"Yeah." Andy nodded. "Yeah, that could be."

"Could be."

"But the tape's gone. How's that gonna help us, Nick? If we could find the tape, fine, but it's gone."

"The others aren't."

"Pardon?" Andy wrinkled up his nose.

Nick passed him another photo. This showed the bookshelves. "No files, hunh?" He traced his finger along a row of bookshelves. "But right along here, all these books look just the same."

"Yeah?"

"But they are not books, Andrew."

"They're not?"

"Look at that open carton on the floor. Imagine it closed and sitting on a bookshelf. It would look just like a book, no?"

Andy gaped.

"And so those books on that row are not books, Andrew, all those books that look the same are *tapes*, just like the box on the floor!"

"Geez, I see it now, I never thought about—"

"Yeah, never thought." Nick snorted. "What's the matter with everybody? You never thought. Our man Shelldrake never thought. The police never thought.

Nobody thinks, nobody sees either. About as hard to see as a fly in a glass of milk. These are the *files*, kid!"

Andy nodded, gagged lightly, and coughed into his fist.

"All right, I want Shelldrake to go back in there."

"You want him to get the tapes?"

"No. That's why you're going into the house with him."

"Me?" Andy was wide-eyed.

"Ri-i-ght." Nick grinned sardonically, gathered up the photos, stuffed them back in the envelopes, and shoved the envelopes into Andy's hands. "It's about time you got a little experience in the skulduggery side of the business, my fine young man. I want Shelldrake to take you in. I want you to listen to those tapes—no time to hear them all, just skip around, take notes, be selective."

Before Andy could respond, another jogger suddenly plopped wearily down at the table.

"Nice time of day to run," he said to Nick.

"Yeah, beautiful."

"You finished?"

"Yeah. But my friend here is just about to get started." He smiled at Andy. "Like, I think you should go home now, change your clothes, meet your jogging partner, and get active."

"Now?" Andy said.

"Right now, before it gets any hotter."

Andy swallowed and nodded, got aboard his bicycle and rode off.

"Not everybody likes to run," the jogger said.

"Not everybody."

"Personally, I'd rather run in the early evening,

you know. When the automatic sprinklers are on, I like to run through 'em. You know, along people's lawns, when you can get away with it."

"Automatic sprinklers?"

"Yeah. You're not from around here. I see your Phillies hat."

"No. People got automatic sprinklers here?"

"Well, in the rich neighborhoods especially. They just come on at a certain time, you know, toward evening, and go off later. Everything's automatic these days."

"Yeah. Everything except human beings." Nick got up and dumped his cup and the rest of his taco in a trash can.

"And dogs," the jogger said. "You gotta watch out for dogs, especially if you run toward night. I got bit last night, that's why I'm running this morning."

"Yeah, dogs. I gotta get to work. Have fun in the sprinklers." Nick ambled off toward his car. He was pensive. Andy was smarter than that, more thorough. He shouldn't have missed those tapes in the photos. Neither should Shelldrake. They needed a kick in the butt. He wondered if maybe he should tell Andy the whole story, about the Justice Department and all. That would prod him into more careful work. But for thet time being, Andy was better left out of that part of it. Safer for the kid.

The courtroom was jammed as usual, as it would be every day of the trial. Selection of the jury was important, and Nick paid careful attention to it, but in this case he didn't think it was crucial.

If this case went to the jury on the basis of the facts as they were now known, they'd convict. It wouldn't matter much who sat on the jury or how skillfully Nick presented the defense. In order to get Lon Braden off, Nick would have to blow the case open with something new.

Still, he had his job to do, so he heeded Anne's questioning of prospective jurors, and questioned them closely himself. Nick used up most of his preemptory challenges quickly, rejecting the son of a Tucson insuranceman; a man who had once won a service award with the JayCees; an elderly woman who listened to the radio all day.

Most of the jury was now empaneled, and Anne was interviewing the latest prospect, a black man, forty-seven, balding, serious. "Mr. Hamlin, have you formed any opinion as to the guilt or innocence of the defendant?"

Hamlin hesitated. "I'm willing to keep an open mind."

Anne nodded to the judge. "Mr. Hamlin is acceptable to the people."

The judge looked over at the defense table. He was a pale, elderly man, with eyebrows so light they blended in with the skin. The robe seemed to weigh heavy on his frail shoulders. "Mr. Hellinger?"

"Mr. Hamlin," Nick began softly as he approached the man in the modern, well-lit courtroom, "have you read any newspaper accounts of this case or watched any coverage on television?"

"Pretty hard not to."

"Have you?"

Hamlin looked wary, as if expecting a trick. "I would have to say yes."

"But you think you could render an impartial verdict."

"Yes, sir, I do."

Nick leaned casually on the low partition enclosing

the witness chair and looked around the courtroom, finally facing the prosecutor's table. Anne avoided his eyes. "Despite the fact that Mr. Braden has been accused of having links with organized crime?"

Anne jumped to her feet, just as Nick had expected. "Your Honor, the people have made no such allegations!"

"Not yet," Nick said quietly. "Strike the question."

Anne sat down. Nick strode back to his table and picked up a note sheet. "You're a religious man, aren't you, Mr. Hamlin? The First Baptist Church?"

"I'm a God-fearing man," Hamlin asserted, "if that's what you mean."

Good. He had piqued the man's sensitivity. "You said you have a son who lives in Canada."

"Yes, sir."

"And you haven't seen him in eleven years. Could you tell me why?"

"He ran away when he was going to be drafted, that's why."

"He avoided the draft, that's why?"

Hamlin fidgeted. "Had nothing to say to him."

"Nothing to say to your son?"

"He made the choice."

"You don't approve of what he did."

"No."

"Is he a religious boy, Mr. Hamlin, like yourself?"

"Don't sound like it, running away."

"Your Honor"—Nick faced the judge—"the defense challenges this juror, for cause."

"On what grounds?" Anne asked quickly, rising.

"He's a little *too* God-fearing for me. Prejudice against human frailty, vindictive self-righteousness, lack of open mind about personal choice—take your pick."

"Objection. Insufficient grounds."

The judge turned his pale eyes toward Nick. "Sustained, Mr. Hellinger. You have one preemptory challenge remaining. Do you wish to use it at this time?"

He had thought the elderly judge might bite on "human frailty." "Yes, Your Honor." He shrugged and sat down. He didn't want this guy, would take a chance on the next one.

Hamlin was excused. Next called was a woman about thirty-five, moderately attractive, chicly dressed. She'd be acceptable, let her be seated; Nick's mind wandered to Andy and Shelldrake. What they were doing now was more important to his case.

Andy was eager to talk, bursting with pride. No, he certainly hadn't broken the case wide open; he had simply done what Nick instructed him to do, and it had excited him enormously.

That night they sat in the hotel suite now refurnished as an office. Surrounded by desks, file cabinets, a copying machine, they sipped coffee from their own automatic brewer. Andy related the tale of what he and Shelldrake had accomplished, leaving out nothing at all—clearly Nick's admonition had left its mark, and he was filled with details.

Shelldrake had outfitted them with coveralls of telephone-company repairmen, and somehow had picked up a company van as well. There was no one else on the street when they arrived at Savage's house. Wearing gloves, they carried toolboxes from the truck. Shelldrake slipped the lock in some mysterious fashion as fast as if he had a key.

They went right to the tapes and the machine. Shelldrake seemed to know how to operate anything. The tapes were numbered and dated. They started from the very first one and worked down the row. Each time, Shelldrake threaded the machine and then went to the window to serve as lookout while the tape played and Andy listened and took notes. By selectively skipping ahead as Nick had directed, Andy was able to note each different character and subject.

"Here's how good he was," Andy said, his eyes bright. "The tape cartons were a little dusty. When he handled them, naturally some of the dust came off. He had a little rubber squirter of some kind, filled with stuff just like dust. And when we were finished, he made them look like nobody had touched them!"

"Yeah, yeah, and I'm sure he left everything just as you had found it, as if nobody had even been in the room."

"Exactly!"

"So he just passed Elementary House Entry, beginner's course." Nick poured more coffee. "So then you left."

"Right." Andy flipped open the topmost of several small notepads. "Now, according to the tapes, we—"

"Anybody on the street when you left?"

"Oh, yeah, right. No. We came out, Shelldrake tested the door to make sure it was locked, then we got into the van. Shelldrake dropped me off downtown. I changed cabs twice." He raised his eyebrows, waiting for approval.

"Fine, fine. So you're here."

"Right. So"—Andy propped his feet up on the desk and looked at his notepad—"based on the tapes, we've narrowed it down to nine possibilities from Savage's pending hit list. Couple of building contractors, a labor organizer, a restaurant supplier, a city councilman—pretty mixed bag."

"Who's talking on the tapes?"

"Hunh?"

"Is it just Savage dictating to himself, or are there other voices on there?"

"Mostly it's just Savage. But occasionally he's on the phone, talking to these others—like trying to trap them into admitting something. That's how we narrowed it down, taking just those he talked directly to. Shelldrake's checking out their alibis. Without police cooperation, though, it won't be easy."

"Is that a fact, Andrew? My, my."

"Well, I mean—"

"No, it ain't gonna be easy! And no, there won't be police cooperation! They already think they've made their case!" Nick stomped around the room. "Tell Shelldrake to hire more manpower, do whatever he has to. The prosecution's case is circumstantial, but persuasive. If we don't turn up something equally persuasive, we're burned." He drew a cup of water from the upside-down bottle and started to drink it. He stopped. "You didn't mention Braden."

"Pardon?"

Nick spun toward him. "You never mentioned Braden on those tapes. Why not?"

"I guess because his name never came up."

"Never came up! Then what the hell was Braden worried about? What was going on?"

"Does seem strange."

"*Strange!* Stranger than strange, my friend. Jesus . . ." Nick scratched his pate.

"Something else, Nick."

"Yeah?" Nick was still trying to make sense out of the last revelation.

"Well, that theory of yours—that when Braden

showed up unexpectedly, the killer panicked and grabbed the tape and reels off the machine to cover himself?"

"Yeah?"

"Well, I don't think it will wash. All the tape cartons on the shelf were numbered. Two more are missing."

Nick stared at him. He continued staring at him as he sat slowly down and fished for a small address book in his pocket. He glanced into the address book, then dialed a number on the phone. "Tell me something, Andrew. My old case, the Delgado case, you remembered trial motions even I'd forgotten. How?"

"I memorized."

"So, your memory's good. Why's it like pulling teeth to get it out of you?" He spoke into the phone. "Rossetti? Hellinger. Off the record, how many tapes did your boys lift from Savage's study?"

Rossetti paused. "Two. Just the stuff he had on Braden, we took 'em for safekeeping. But how did you—"

Nick hung up. He smiled at Andy's mystified expression. "Don't worry about it, kid, it'll put lines in that young face. All right, I'll explain it to you."

They sat up late. Nick did not tell him all of it, just enough so that he could see what was riding on the case. He did not mention the Justice Department, just said that Braden was a fink for the government, and they needed him alive.

Then they discussed the trial and how it would go.

"Gronouski will put on the arresting officers first and go through that number," Nick said, "then probably this Laura Weire that you talked to, to bring up the so-called threats."

"What about the defense?"

"We've got nothing, Andrew, as of now. Can't

even put Braden on the stand. Essentially I'll be dragging it out, playing for time until we come up with something."

"I thought you wanted a quick trial, because of the risks of leaks and all."

"Yeah. We're walking a tightrope. Keep that in mind."

The courtroom seemed warm. Nick couldn't tell if it was because the air-conditioning was on the blink, or because he still wasn't quite used to the weather, or because he was nervous. In the back, Cara Braden too dabbed at her neck with a handkerchief. The jurors sat primly in the box, as if afraid to move.

On the witness stand next to the pale judge was Laura Weire, Paul Savage's young assistant. They seemed to be cut from a mold, these young TV women, Nick thought. All pretty, slender, serious. Lon Braden sat between Nick and Andy, his eyes like theirs on Anne and Laura Weire.

"And then," Anne said, "you saw Mr. Braden enter the television studio?"

"Yes. He walked right onto the set."

"And he spoke to you."

"Yes. He wanted to know where Mr. Savage was. I am always under strict orders about that, so naturally I didn't tell him."

"What did he say—his exact words, if you can remember them?"

Miss Weire thought for a moment. "He said something about he would sue Paul—Mr. Savage—with a million-dollar lawsuit. And then he said, 'if I don't strangle him first.'"

"Those were his exact words—'if I don't strangle him first'?"

"Yes."

"Then what happened?"

"Our assistant director mentioned that Mr. Savage was still at home. I was frightened. Mr. Braden looked mad enough to—"

"Objection!" Nick was on his feet.

"Sustained," the judge said quietly. "Strike that last remark."

Anne took a deep breath. "You said you were frightened."

"Yes, I was," Laura said firmly, glancing over at Braden.

"Why?"

"Mr. Braden rushed out, and I thought he would be going to Mr. Savage's house. And if you knew how Mr. Savage felt about that . . ."

"What, if anything, did you do at that point?"

She gulped, spoke hesitantly. "I tried to call Paul, to warn him. But . . . the receiver was off the hook. The line was busy, and Mr. Savage often took the phone off the hook when he didn't want to be disturbed. Then I . . ." She gulped again, tears formed in her eyes. "I called the police. I was afraid. They sent a squad car. But it was . . . too late . . ." She put her hands to her eyes.

"No further questions," Anne said softly.

Nick waited for the girl to compose herself, then approached her. "Miss Weire, was Mr. Braden to be mentioned by name on that evening's broadcast?"

"Yes. To the best of my knowledge."

"You weren't certain?"

"Mr. Savage often changed plans at the last minute. He didn't always tell me."

"If he was to be mentioned, what would have been the context of that? In what connection was he to be mentioned?"

"I couldn't say for sure. I would assume it had to do with Mr. Braden's association with Clinton Tolliver."

"You would *assume?*"

Laura sniffed, then straightened. "Mr. Savage was doing a series on organized crime," she said stiffly. "The focus of his current investigation was Trans-Texas Industries, of which Clinton Tolliver is the president."

Nick was glad she had pulled herself together. Nothing worked against you more than a weepy opposition witness. She got nicely starchy when she turned to the business of the TV show. He pulled out his pocket watch, snapped open the case to see the face, snapped it shut, put it back in his pocket. "Miss Weire, from whom did Mr. Savage obtain his information?"

"I don't know." She looked quickly at Anne Gronouski, who seemed on the verge of rising.

"Oh, really?" Nick panned his eyes over the jurors. "Week after week, your boss dishes up the latest dirt on Houston's seamy underside, and *you,* his assistant, don't know where it came from?"

"Objection!" Anne was on her feet. "Argumentative, Your Honor."

"If it please the court," Nick said, moving away from the witness stand, "the prosecution contends that the imminent disclosure of his name on television led Alonzo Braden to commit murder. If that is so, then *anyone* subject to exposure on the broadcast had the same motive. Yet we don't know for sure that Mr. Braden was to be mentioned, or who if anybody else. I submit that where Mr. Savage got his information, from whom, is crucial to discovery of who was to be exposed."

"Your Honor," Anne snapped back, "Mr. Hellinger is attempting to cloud the issue with phantom suspects. And the witness has already answered that she didn't know who the source was."

"Objection sustained," the judge said.

All right, he had got that into the jurors' heads anyway. And for a moment drawn their attention away from the witness. He had to be careful with the pretty Miss Weire. He wanted to have her testy, defending the TV show, but didn't want her breaking down.

He turned to her again. "Would it be fair to say, Miss Weire, that you were kept pretty much in the dark about the show?"

"I wouldn't say I was in the dark. I was Paul's assistant, after all. I was responsible for a great deal, including—"

"Let me make sure that I remember your testimony correctly." He paced thoughtfully in front of the jury. "You don't know the identity of Savage's sources. You don't know for sure what was going on the broadcast that night, but you *assume* it had to do with Clinton Tolliver. You've testified that the defendant threatened to strangle Paul Savage." He looked at her with a slight smile that he hid from the jury. "But one cannot both strangle and then sue the deceased, can one? So, Miss Weire, wouldn't it seem logical to you that these words were used to express quite normal and nonlethal frustration over not being able to get in touch with your boss? After all, didn't you say that Mr. Braden came to the studio specifically hoping to *find* Mr. Savage there? Did you suppose he intended to dispatch Mr. Savage right there on the set, amid the crew members? Isn't it true that you were 'afraid,' as you put it, only because if Mr. Savage were disturbed, he would be angry with you for having allowed that to happen? I would think that—"

"Your Honor." Anne got wearily to her feet. "Defense isn't cross-examining this witness, he's delivering a summation!"

"Was I?" Nick looked innocently at Anne, then the judge. "Forgive me. No further questions." He had got away with a lot, considering Anne's alertness. As he returned to his seat, a uniformed officer came down the aisle and handed her a note.

She opened the note. Nick was sure she suddenly paled, but she recovered quickly.

"Your Honor?"

"Yes, Miss Gronouski?"

"It's nearly four. Rather than begin with the next witness, I wonder if we might adjourn at this time?"

"All right with you, Mr. Hellinger?"

"Fine, Your Honor."

"Very well, then." The judge picked up the gavel—with some effort, it seemed. "This court stands adjourned until ten o'clock tomorrow morning." He banged the gavel, rose clumsily, and left the bench.

Nick watched Anne. He thought her voice had been shaky in asking for the adjournment. Now she quickly packed up and raced out of the courtroom.

"What's that all about?" Andy asked, puzzled by Anne's flight.

"Who knows? Maybe they caught a crook."

CHAPTER 8

THE TRIAL dragged on through subsequent days with obvious witnesses—people from the TV studio, the taxi driver who delivered Braden to Savage's, a crime-lab technician—none of the testimony new, none of it surprising. If the jury and spectators had expected theatrics, they weren't getting much, not from either side.

Nick thought Anne had changed lately. Earlier so sober and professional and alert, now she seemed distracted. It was not something an ordinary attendant at the trial would notice. But she had become a bit more mechanical, a bit less sharp.

He was puzzled as well by the police. They could have done a more thorough job checking out clues much like Nick—through Andy and Shelldrake—had done. Maybe they were just overconfident. That was fine with Nick. Sometimes cases swung his way because of sloppy or insufficient police work.

Lon Braden was holding up well, worried but quiet about it. He tried to carry on a somewhat normal life with his family. Toughest of all right now for Lon, Nick thought, might be in keeping the salient facts of his involvement secret from his wife. That took a lot. There was no mistaking how close they were in every other way.

Nick and Lon stood at the rail on the upper level of the Galleria, watching the activity on the skating rink below.

The rink was crowded. Cara and Julie skated in the company of another mother and daughter. Julie was a determined, if unaccomplished, skater. She fell, quickly regained her feet, glanced sheepishly up to her father.

Braden gave her the thumbs-up.

"You kind of like that kid, hunh?"

"She'll do." Braden smiled.

"Her old lady's not too bad either."

"Easy for you to say, you don't have to eat her meatloaf." He waited for Nick's chuckle, then nodded. "She's super, Nick. Unbelievably supportive and trusting, never complains. I hate what this is doing to her. I hate not being able to—"

"Daddy! Look!" Julie was making a slow, uneven figure on the ice.

"I'm watching, baby!" Braden called down.

"Lon, I've heard it from Rossetti," Nick said, "but not from you. Why'd you get involved in all of this?"

"Rossetti's boys picked me up at college, he's probably told you all about that."

"He told me. But I couldn't quite figure the motivation for something as risky as this."

"Well, there's stuff Rossetti doesn't know. I don't talk about it."

"Talk about it to me."

Braden shrugged. "It's in the genes, I guess. My father was a union organizer. A kind of road-company Samuel Gompers. It was tough for unionizers in those days."

"I know something about those days."

"Well, my father hated the sweat shops, the conditions, the moguls getting rich by chewing up little people. For him, it was the union first, the union last, the union forever. It was his life."

"An admirable life. You must've been proud."

"Yeah, I was. But it was his death, too. One day, they moved in and took it over—the goons, the wise guys. You know, the companies would hire these fake union guys, set them up like a competing union, and send them in to disrupt the real union. My father knew what was happening. He took them on."

"Very dangerous."

"Yeah, and lonely. Not too many would stand up, they didn't dare. But my father stood up. They took care of him, of course."

"How?"

Braden scuffed his feet and looked away. His voice was choked. "He didn't die right away. It would've been a mercy if he had. The guys with the lead pipes left him breathing. He hung on for as long as he could in the hospital, wired up to tubes and machines. When he could talk, he'd say, 'I'll get the bastards.' But he couldn't talk much. Then one day it all stopped. The machines couldn't save him."

Nick watched him fighting back the tears—queer

kinship the two of them had, lawyer and client, after all.

When he spoke again, his voice was clear and steady. "I'm no hero, Nick. I'm just my father's son."

"Cara know about that?"

"The bare bones of it. But I never made it a big deal, never allowed it to seem related to my career or anything."

"And for ten years you've let her go on thinking that you're Tolliver's boy."

"What would you have done?"

"I don't know. I don't know if I'd be tough enough."

"I didn't expect to get this involved, didn't expect it to go on so long. It was like I got sucked in deeper and deeper."

"And then the Justice Department had you in their grip just as surely as if they were the mob."

"Just about the same. I was on the right side, but I was trapped in it. I had to depend on them to protect me. And the only way out was to follow the whole thing through. We go so close. Then this . . ."

"She's a tough lady, your wife."

"You don't know the half of it. How scared she's been—not even knowing I was feeding the government under cover, just thinking I was involved with those vicious Tolliver bastards. And if I'd have told her the truth, she'd have been even more scared. She'd be a partner in my nightmares."

"Daddy!"

"Hey, look, Nick, a figure eight!"

In the middle of it, Julie fell.

"Well, a seven and a half." He called down, "Try it again, Julie!"

Nick regarded him. Julie's father, Cara's husband, this man lonely with his secret life. What hell it must be not to share so desperate a situation with those closest to him.

"So," Braden said, "how you think things are going so far?"

Nick wanted to protect him. But to be anything but open and honest at the same time would be a condescension unworthy of him. "I've gotta be straight with you, Lon. It doesn't look all that good."

"No, hunh?"

"Don't misunderstand me, we're not beaten by a long shot, I got certain people out there digging for me, and your innocence is on our side. But the most important ingredient of all right now is off limits."

"Me."

"Yeah. You'd be committing perjury the minute you took the stand."

"I know." Braden watched his wife and daughter below. "So you'll just do the best you can with what you've got, right?"

So gentle and tender a plea, when the man's life was at stake.

"I'm fighting all the way, and I am a very tough man to beat. I just wanted you to know..."

"I know."

"Right now the best thing I can do is get back to work. Get some sleep, Lon. Hug Julie for me."

Those times with Braden when Nick had nothing encouraging to report were excrutiating. The trial, the investigating, the concern for the Braden family—Nick was beginning to feel drained. In his occupation, he often had to walk the fine line between working enough and working too much. He couldn't afford to go into the courtroom exhausted, he had to be alert every minute.

Similarly demanding of his full attention was balancing the activities of Rossetti and Tolliver as well as those of Manolo Shelldrake. He thought of Anne, too, and hoped she had straightened things out with her daughter, but that looked like something that would take some time to correct.

Too bad about Anne. Under other circumstances, they might have found mutual comfort together.

Nick hated hotel rooms, but in this situation, there was comfort in the neutrality of the plastic furnishings, the dull walls and carpet, the drab pastel seascapes. For some reason, he was able to relax in such a nondescript environment.

He switched on the TV, opened a bottle of Lone Star beer, and settled back on the bed to watch the news.

It was the lead story, as usual. Nick recognized the reporter from his press conference with Graebner.

". . . As the Savage murder trial entered its sixth day, Lieutenant Forrest Shavers of the Houston Police Crime Lab confirmed that fingerprints found on the windowsill and on the phone in the Savage residence were those of the defendant, Alonzo Braden . . ."

Yeah, yeah, *prints*. As if he'd denied being there, as if that's all the cops had to check to make a case.

". . . Once again Assistant District Attorney Anne Gronouski attempted to introduce testimony linking Braden to alleged crime boss Clinton Tolliver, a tactic which the defendant's counsel, noted Philadelphia attorney Nicholas Hellinger, once again successfully defeated . . ."

Noted Philadelphia attorney—like a goddamned broken record. Might as well say "self-admitted" if they really wanted to stick him with alien status. But Anne kept trying to sneak that in about the mob link. That's why Nick beat her to the punch in the examination of jurors, by asserting that she *would* try to bring it in. Odd she stuck with it because he was going to knock it out every time.

"... Following today's proceedings, I managed to catch Defense Attorney Hellinger for a couple of quick questions."

They ran the film showing Nick in the court corridor with the TV reporter next to him, microphone in hand. Other reporters crowded around.

"Mr. Hellinger," the reporter said in the film, "can you tell us how you think it's going?"

"Slowly."

Just right, make it look as if he was not holding things up.

The reporter waited for him to elaborate, Nick didn't. Then he asked, "Earlier you made references to some sort of mysterious informant. What did you mean by that?"

"What I meant was no mystery, I made it clear in the courtroom. *Somebody* was feeding Savage his dirt. He sure didn't dig the [*bleep*] out of the [*bleep*] Yellow Pages."

The press would wince when he used profanities, but he knew they loved him for it. Nick Hellinger made good copy—or good listening, anyway.

The reporter persisted: "Does this mean you have reason to believe that this informant may be connected to the slaying?"

"What I'm saying is that I believe the information Savage was receiving may have something to do with the crime. If the informant himself is not involved, he sure as [*bleep*] could give us a lead on who might be."

The film showed Nick trying to move ahead through the crowd of reporters. Others tried to get at him with questions, but one reporter shouldered them away.

"Assistant DA Gronouski intends to call Detective Donovan to the stand tomorrow . . ."

"That's my understanding."

"His testimony could prove extremely damaging to your client. Does this worry you?"

"No. My client's innocent. The more facts we can bring out, the better shot we've got at demonstrating his innocence. Know what would really worry me?" He stopped and turned to the reporter, giving him a cocky smile. "If Miss Gronouski *didn't* call Sergeant Donovan to the stand."

The film ended, the news went on to other subjects. Nick opened another beer and vacantly watched the assessment of the world situation.

Anne would have nothing new to present. In fact, maybe she herself was worried about Donovan. She certainly couldn't avoid putting him on the stand. But as smart as she was, she would have to be aware that Detective Sergeant Donovan had performed a pretty sloppy investigation. Sloppy enough, at least, to give noted Philadelphia Attorney Nicholas Hellinger a chance to make some waves.

Maybe that was what was bothering her lately.

There was a knock at the door. Nick turned his head toward it without answering. Another knock, quiet, brief like the first.

"Yeah?" Nick called.

Three more quick taps.

Nick sighed, hauled himself off the bed, and went to the door. He did not open it. "Yeah, who's there?"

A note was slid under the door. Nick picked it up and opened it. "Mr. Hellinger: Got important information for you. Must talk."

Well, Nick thought, nobody's gunning for me on either side, as far as I know. Only real trouble out there could be the murderer himself, and he would not come here—unless he was totally crazy, of course.

A break was needed; it was worth a chance.

Without removing the safety chain, Nick cracked the door open and peeked out.

Standing there nervously looking right and left was a sallow man of slight build, wearing a straw cowboy hat pulled low over his eyes, a cheap, ill-fitting gray suit, yellowing white shirt with string tie, and scuffed cowboy boots.

"You got something for me?" Nick said quietly.

"Please, quick, let me come in. I don't wanna be seen out here."

Birdlike hands, scrawny neck, sharp nose, bad teeth. Nothing the guy could do without a gun, and he didn't look like a quick-draw type. Nick could break that neck first.

He undid the chain and let the man step in. Nick stayed close to him.

"Mr. Hellinger."

"What's on your mind? Make it quick, I got people coming up."

"Five minutes, that's all I need"—he splayed out his fingers—"five."

"I'm counting."

"Well, see . . ." The man's eyes darted around. "Can we sit down?"

"No. Talk."

"Well, see, I was kinda wanderin' in that neighborhood, see, 'round the Savage place—I kind of like to keep an eye on things, certain neighborhoods . . ."

"Get to it, friend, three minutes and counting."

Suddenly he blurted, "I seen the killing, Mr. Hellinger, I *seen* it! I was out in the back, behind the wall, I heard this ruckus, I crept up. I seen this fight. Then I beat it outta there. But I seen it."

The guy looked like a rat, acted like one. Nick kept just enough distance to make a quick move to him with either hand. "Who?"

"Braden. That guy on trial. He done it. I seen it. Nobody seen it but me. Nobody knows it but me, and now you."

Nick's left hand shot up from his belt to the neck of the small man. He grabbed his collar and began to tighten. The man's eyes bulged. His hat fell off.

"I can lift you right to the ceiling like this," Nick growled. "What's your play, punk? Spill it!"

"Leggo," the man gasped, grabbing for Nick's hand. "Leggo..."

Nick relaxed the grip, but kept his hand on the collar.

The man gasped, shook his head, put his hand to his neck. "A deal, that's all."

Be a favor to the world to break this guy's neck. Nick clenched his teeth, said nothing.

"See, I din't wanna go to the police or nobody with it, 'cause I rather help you. I thought maybe it was worth somethin' to you, if I din't."

"Like what?"

The man moved his lips soundlessly, then managed, "Maybe couple grand?"

Nick tightened his grip fiercely.

"Couple hunnert!" the man gagged, clawing at Nick's hand.

Nick twisted the collar, the man's face was beet red. "How about five bucks, hunh? Still too high for me." He slowly lifted the man. The man danced frantically on his toes, his face turned blue. "Well, the price is going down, punk, 'cause you didn't see horseshit!" The man's mouth hung open, saliva dribbled down his wiggling jaw from his protruding tongue. "You know what it's worth to try and hustle me?" With his other hand, Nick separated a dollar bill from the roll in his pocket, wadded it up, and jammed it into the man's mouth. Then he flung him across the room against the door.

The man slammed into it backward, then slid slowly down it into a sitting position, the crinkled dollar sticking out between his lips like a snake's tongue, his eyes bulging like a bass.

Nick picked up the hat and delicately placed it on the man's head. "That buck will get you on a bus. You go as far as you can on that. And then you get off and run. You run as far and fast as you can. Because if I ever see you around this town I'll unscrew that head of yours and stick it where the sun don't shine. You got three seconds to disappear!" He booted the man aside and yanked open the door.

The man tried to scramble to his feet, half-crawling through the door, and stumbled off down the hall and around the corner.

For easing tension, Nick mused, contemplating a broken fingernail, that beats jogging.

Roy Donovan intrigued Nick. He had a good reputation as a tough, street-savvy detective. If sometimes he bent the rules a little, he got the job done. Like a lot of good detectives, he was a man about whose methods and successes Nick had mixed feelings. He sympathized with them for the difficulties and dangers and legal complexities of their jobs. The thing he liked about the good ones was that, even if they snuck around behind the law a little, they generally were after the right guy for the right reason.

So, was Donovan getting a little lazy? Thinking early retirement, maybe? Whatever, he was Nick's best hope so far for shaking the case, and he was anxious for Anne to finish so he could get at the calm detective with the sneering face.

Donovan had run down his initial involvement in the case, and was finishing up in response to Anne's questioning.

"... So I arrived at the scene at approximately nine-fifteen p.m. The arresting officers had the suspect in their car with them. They reported to me what they had found, whereupon I ordered that the suspect be taken to the station and booked on suspicion of murder."

"No further questions," Anne said.

Odd place to end it, Nick thought as Anne sat down, because Donovan remained on the scene to investigate. She had questioned his subordinates more closely than him about the subsequent investigation. Anne stared off, rolling a pencil back and forth between her palms. She seemed to be concentrating marginally at best, but seemed nonetheless anxious rather than casual—puzzling.

Donovan watched with his strange half-smile as Nick approached the stand. Nick turned his serious eyes on the jury.

"Now, Detective Donovan, according to your report, the defendant stated that when he entered the residence, the back door was already standing open, right?"

"That's correct."

"He further stated that inasmuch as he'd heard the sound of quarreling from inside the study moments before, it was obvious that he'd just missed encountering the fleeing murderer, right?" Still he didn't look at Donovan.

"Correct."

Abruptly Nick faced him. "Why didn't you look into this, Detective Donovan?"

"Why didn't I?"

"Clearly, there was only one escape route available to the killer—across the backyard." He anticipated an objection from Anne for not letting Donovan answer the prior question, but she was silent. "The sprinklers were on. The ground was soaked." He turned to the jury again. "There could've been fresh footprints, perhaps a scrap of cloth torn from the killer's clothing when he scrambled over the wall—something. Yet you did *nothing?*"

"I didn't say I did nothing."

"You checked for footprints in the lawn, and the wall for evidence? Your report doesn't mention that."

"My report describes how I traced the defendant's movements during the afternoon and evening to the point of arrest. There was no reason to case the entire neighborhood. I had my man."

"Did you?" Nick raised his eyebrows dubiously to the jury.

"I did. And he's sitting right—"

"You were *that* positive?"

"Correct."

Nick paced up and down in front of the jury, rubbing his chin. "Suppose—just suppose, Detective Donovan—that the defendant were to be acquitted. Always possible, no? If that happened, you'd have one helluva time developing a new investigation from such a cold trail."

"Acquittal doesn't mean a man's innocent," Donovan muttered.

Nick spun toward him. "I don't remember asking you that question, Detective Donovan!"

The judge blinked his pale eyes and nodded. "The witness will please confine himself to answering the questions put by counsel."

"Thank you, Your Honor. But let it stand. Okay, what you say is true. The law is designed to protect as well as to convict, however. So while acquittal doesn't prove innocence, neither does circumstantial evidence prove guilt. And it is guilt, not innocence, that must be proved in a court of law, isn't that correct, Detective Donovan?

Donovan, caught off-balance, shrugged.

"Pardon?"

"Yes."

"Yes," Nick repeated more loudly. "So let us examine circumstances in a slightly larger context. Tell me, Detective Donovan, before his arrest had you ever met Alonzo Braden?"

Donovan hesitated. "No."

"I'm sure a routine check you must have carried out revealed that he had no prior arrests of any kind, am I right?"

"That's correct."

"In fact, I'm sure you found nothing to contradict the premise that he was a law-abiding taxpayer, a good family man, and in every sense a credit to the community."

Nick had casually baited the hook. Donovan squirmed, and bit.

"He was more of a credit to..." His voice dropped, but he couldn't quite catch himself in time. "...Tolliver's mob."

"Oh really?" Nick jumped in quickly, not giving him a breather. "In other words, were it not for my client's alleged association with characters you personally consider unsavory—allegations not hitherto even admitted to the record of this trial—you might have entertained the possibility that he was actually telling the truth."

"No, that's not what I—"

"And if you had conceded that possibility, might you not have performed the job that the good citizens of Houston have every right to expect from you?"

"What?" Donovan looked confused.

"Let me rephrase the question." Nick kept moving fast. The pale old judge didn't have a chance to react, and Anne didn't move. "Since your only suspect in the case has steadfastly maintained his innocence, and since there is nothing to link him directly to the crime except his presence near the scene, did you proceed to examine the scene with an eye toward discovering further evidence, even if such evidence might point toward another suspect?"

"I did my job!" Donovan snapped, sneering.

Nick hoped the jury would see the expression as one of petulance, like a child, like a boy caught sneaking away from his homework. "Indeed?" He started toward his table. "Then why is there no mention in your report of a missing recording tape?"

Andy proudly handed Nick a photo. Nick looked at it, nodded, then looked casually at the judge. "There's a question pending, Your Honor."

Donovan didn't wait. "What tape?"

"I have a photograph, taken at the crime scene by one of your—"

Finally the judge's gavel cut him off—Nick knew it couldn't last forever. "Miss Gronouski?"

She looked up at the bench.

"If you do not intend to offer an objection . . ."

"Yes, excuse me. I do object, Your Honor."

Nick wondered if she had been following at all.

The judge nodded. "Mr. Hellinger, you're familiar with the rules of evidence. If you have an exhibit, introduce it in the proper fashion."

"Yes, Your Honor. And excuse *me*." Nick flourished the photograph. "If it please the court, I request that this photo be marked Defense Exhibit 'A.'"

"So ordered."

The clerk marked it, entered it in his log, and returned it. Nick showed it to Anne, who nodded cursorily, then to Donovan. Donovan took it reluctantly.

"I ask you to study this picture, detective, specifically the tape recorder and the area immediately adjacent to it, and tell the jury what you see."

Donovan stared dully at the photo. "I see a tape recorder."

Some titters came from the spectators.

Nick nodded, unsmiling. "Do you see a tape on the tape recorder?"

Apparently encouraged by the audience, Donovan answered, "No, I do not see a tape on the tape recorder."

"Do you see a take-up reel on the tape recorder—please answer yes or no."

"No."

"But next to the tape recorder"—Nick looked deadpan at the jury—"you see an empty tape box, do you not?"

"I see a box."

"What do you suppose happened to the tape reel it contained?"

"How should I know?"

"Well, let's see." Nick rubbed his chin. "How

would a detective know? Did the defendant have it on his person when he was arrested?"

"No."

"Did it turn up any place else in your investigation?"

"No."

"No? Then *where is it?*"

Donovan squirmed and looked up at the judge who rapped his gavel.

"Miss Gronouski," the judge said wearily, "do you persist on relying upon me?"

Again she looked surprised. "No, Your Honor. Unh, proper introduction of evidence . . ."

The judge heaved a sigh and directed his attention to Nick. "Is it your intention, counselor, to introduce this tape into evidence?"

"If only I could," Nick said sorrowfully. "Unfortunately, it is my belief that the killer took it."

"A belief yet to be substantiated in any way." He cocked an eye at Anne, who seemed not inclined to carry on what the judge had initiated. "Do you have first-hand knowledge as to the contents of the supposedly missing tape, Mr. Hellinger, or even evidence of its existence? And beyond that, can you demonstrate that it even bears upon this trial?"

"No, Your Honor. Just my belief."

"Then until you do have the proper foundation—your belief aside—I ask you to confine yourself to proper cross-examination." He gave both Nick and Anne a rather sour look. "It's nearly four-thirty. And since I'm sure, Mr. Hellinger, that you have many more questions to put to this witness, might I suggest that we—"

"Forgive me, Your Honor, but I'm nearly finished."

The judge appeared mildly surprised, arching his almost invisible eyebrows; Donovan showed relief. But Nick figured he'd pushed it about far enough with Donovan—however inattentive Anne might be, the judge was now aroused. Maybe if Donovan could be left with at least a burr in his ass, something to prick him into action, there was still a chance he would go find the real murderer . . .

"Very well," the judge said, "proceed."

Nick addressed Donovan from several feet away, looking at him directly, a proper lecturing mode and distance. "You've served the Houston Police Department for fourteen years, Detective Donovan," Nick said earnestly—relying with confidence on his memorization of facts the night before—"during which time you've earned the reputation of being a superb investigative cop. Since joining homicide, you've handled fifty-three murders, all but six of them resulting in arrests. Thanks to your tireless efforts, convictions have been obtained in over eighty percent of your cases, which the district attorney's office describes as well above the norm."

Donovan was wary, and squirmed under the praise.

"Given these impressive statistics, Detective Donovan, aren't you just a little bit embarrassed by how little ground you covered in your investigation of the Savage killing?"

"No!"

"Wouldn't you like to have more facts?"

"No!"

"Interesting. No further questions." Nick turned on his heel and went to his table, leaving Donovan stunned by his own too-hasty response.

The judge recessed the trial until Monday morning.

"Wipe that gloating grin off your face," Nick said

quietly to Andy. "That was just fancy footwork, it didn't really get us anywhere. Lon, Cara is waiting, I'll talk to you later."

Anne was packing her attaché case. Nick's eyes on her increased her nervousness, and she dropped a file which spilled over the floor.

Nick hurried over and stopped beside her to help collect the papers.

"Hey, lady," he whispered hoarsely, "you could've blown me out of the water all afternoon. What the hell's the matter?"

"You don't know, right?" she whispered back angrily, through clenched teeth.

"No, I don't."

"Hell you don't!" She threw the whispered words like punches.

"I want to talk to you. Wait outside, in your car."

She closed her attaché case, turned her back on him, and stalked out of the courtroom.

The room emptied, Nick packed up his papers, and started out. Donovan stepped in through the rear doors, glanced around, then confronted him, his habitual sneer not menacing now.

"Okay, Mr. Hellinger, you think I'm not doing my job. You think I'm dogging this one, right? Or was that just courtroom theatrics?"

"Donovan," Nick said weariy, "school's out. Get yourself a fishing rod. I hear the perch are biting."

"Wait a minute, listen now. You got any decent leads, anything at all that points to Braden's innocence, just pass it along. I'll follow up if I have to do it on my own time, and that's a promise!"

Something almost desperate in his voice. Nick studied him. "You'll forgive my asking, but why the sudden interest?"

"Not sudden. I'm a native Texan, Mr. Hellinger, and proud of it. We catch enough bad press in the natural scheme of things without some Yankee lawyer claiming we bought a rope before we even heard the verdict."

"Yeah, well, my job's to try to poke holes in your case, and it's already a Swiss cheese. You picked the wrong case to get sloppy on, sergeant. Yankee or no, if your Texas talents can't solve it, my fine Philadelphia nose will. Hey"—he flashed a broad smile and spread his arms grandly—"we're both after justice, right? You'll excuse me..." He brushed past the detective who could only glare at him.

CHAPTER 9

SHE WAS not there, her car was not in the official lot. He stood looking around, maybe he'd get a glimpse of her driving away.

Andy spotted him and came over. "Hey, Nick, that was really fascinating in there. What you looking for?"

"Gronouski. Yeah, it was fascinating, all right. Like walking into a minefield."

"But you were terrific. Boy, the way you pinned Donovan to the—"

"What I was doing was a long way from turning this case around, kid. Like I tried to tell you in there, the jury's not going to wave a happy bye-bye to Braden just because the detective in charge of the case skipped a few steps. Terrific, you think I was? Gronouski was just letting me run free. She should've been on her feet twenty times, objecting. But she wasn't."

"Maybe she's just not quick enough, maybe you overestimated her."

"Heh, heh, you think so? Let me tell you something, Andrew. That lady is as quick as they come. I don't like it. Somebody is setting a trap for me in there, and I don't like it at all."

"Trap? What kind of trap?"

"I don't know."

Andy was more confused than ever. Nick clapped him on the back. "Relax, kid, I'll find out. And you'll be the first to know."

Nick drove to Braden's. Cara met him at the door.

"I want to talk to Lon alone, okay?"

"Sure." She let him in, called her husband, and left them alone in the room.

Nick expected Braden to come in all smiles, as impressed as Andy had been by what had gone on in the courtroom. But he underestimated the accountant. Braden was somber.

"Strange day, Nick, hunh?"

"Yeah."

"And from the looks of your face, you don't like it either."

"I do not. Gronouski wasn't doing her job. Something has happened. You got any ideas?"

"What would I know?"

"I hesitate to ask."

"Hey, Nick"—Lon put a hand on his arm and looked unwaveringly into his eyes—"you think there's maybe something I'm not telling you? Be a little late now for me to clam up, wouldn't it? My life's in your hands every which way."

"Okay, so you thought it was strange too. What

did it look like to you—make a guess."

Lon looked away, rubbed his ear, then looked back. "Pressure."

"My thought exactly."

"Well, assuming right now I was in a position to advise those characters you so niftily called 'unsavory' "—Lon gave Nick a grim little smile—"I would tell them it would be stupid, far too risky, to put pressure on this prosecutor. Now, Tolliver is not always the brightest light on the block, but he's seldom outright clumsy, so I think he personally would steer clear of that kind of thing in this instance. But you know how it is in an outfit like that; everybody around him is trying to suck up, do things they *think* he might like done. They are not as bright as Tolliver. So then, if I were in *your* shoes . . ."

"Say no more." Nick turned for the door. "I don't want anybody to think you're smart enough to run this case."

They exchanged smiles.

It was ironic, Nick thought during the long drive into the cattle country, that right now he was more concerned with the cops and prosecutor doing their jobs than he was with the specifics of the defense. But this was a weird and paradoxical case. He would still win it—Shelldrake might come up with something, a tip might come in from somewhere; Donovan might get off his butt and dig a little deeper, now that he had been so directly, publicly challenged.

Strange dude, that Donovan. Come begging to Nick for anything the defense might turn up that would swing the case. Not like the tough, case-hardened detective his reputation made him out to be. Not so cool, Donovan.

And every now and then the disquieting recognition intruded—if by some magic Nick won the case, got Braden off, it decidedly would be mixed marks for his career. While Nick's reputation for skillful criminal defense would be enhanced, his reputation for ethical standards in acceptance of clients would not. Nick had always drawn the line at defending anything close to mob interests—guilt or innocence notwithstanding.

Win or lose, it would look as if he were in this one for the money, however tainted. And there was no way he could defend himself against the conclusions the public, and other lawyers, would draw.

The only one person with whom he would be able to share the whole story was Judge Carroll, and then only when it was all over. The judge would doubtless be sympathetic to Nick's predicament, the forces he had to contend with. But one thing that the brilliant old curmudgeon would not be sympathetic to was if Nick lost the case.

Ah, me, Nick mused grimly as he entered a series of dirt roads that sent a plume of dust up behind the car; if only hard-nosed Detective Sergeant Roy Donovan had done his usual job from the beginning—had done some real investigating...

Tolliver's ranch, at least that segment he could see near the main house and corrals, had been transformed. Several huge, colorful tents had been erected, hundreds of men milled around them. The corrals were filled with cattle.

Leo met the car and silently led Nick over to a bar under one of the tents where Tolliver was hoisting drinks and holding court. Nick stood at the edge of the crowd and waited for Leo to get the man.

Tolliver looked over, waved, and threaded his way

through the crowd, pausing here and there to slap backs, shake hands. Two husky, stone-faced men followed him.

"Nick!" He stuck out his big free hand from a long way off and held it out as he approached. His other big hand held his drink. "Come on over here, I'll buy you a drink. You may remember my sidekicks here, Jesse and Calvin." He indicated the unsmiling men who stood a few yards back, legs apart.

"Bodyguards, yeah."

"Sidekicks."

"Let's talk, Tolliver."

"Sure, but wouldn't you first like to—"

"No. And leave your goons behind. Leo's enough. We're not even going to arm-wrestle."

"Well, all right, sure, we can talk for a minute." As they walked along the side of a corral where the crowded cattle were bumping together easily, dipping their horns, snorting, pawing the dirt, Tolliver turned and gestured. "This here you're seeing is a real-life cattle auction, Nick, and not an ordinary one neither. No, sir, these pens hold some of the most expensive beefsteak this side of Hollywood. Those cattlemen under the tents come from all over, and their money comes from further than that."

"I'm impressed."

Tolliver's face clouded over. "What I'm tellin' you, Nick, is that some very important business is going on here. I mean to be gracious, but I can't afford to be hustled away from my friends for a long confab."

"I have some important business too, and how long it takes depends on you."

"Shoot," Tolliver said, putting one booted foot up on the fence rail.

"Tolliver, you're much too bright to be stupid, so for the moment I'm going to assume you're not personally responsible for putting the squeeze on the assistant district attorney."

"Squeeze?" Tolliver looked sincerely puzzled. "I got the best attorney in the country gonna get my man off. What you talkin' about, squeeze?"

"Pressure, maybe threats."

"What? She tell you that?"

"She didn't have to tell me. I can see it in the courtroom, feel it. I think somebody's trying to get to her. So I'm asking."

"So I'm answering, since you came straight to me to ask." Tolliver shook his head in amusement. "Threaten a DA? Hard to take you seriously, Nick. *Buy* one, sure—maybe there'd be an occasion now and then to cut through some red tape. But *threaten?* I'm not young enough to be naive nor old enough to be batty. Hell, if it were that easy, the jails would be empty."

"So far I'm buying, about you."

"Be disappointed in you if you didn't."

"But I was thinking that maybe one of your stooges, looking to pile up some brownie points, might be stupid enough." Nick glanced back at Leo.

Tolliver noticed the look, and shook his head. "No way. I got them all paper-trained, house-broke. They don't part their hair different without a direct word from me. And *my* law out here don't need a court, not a lawyer, judge, or cop."

Nick let a discouraged sigh whistle between his teeth. It was still possible Tolliver didn't know, and that one of his men was pulling something, but he wasn't a boss his men would dare cross. Yet, Tolliver also trusted Braden. Hard to figure.

Tolliver clapped him on the shoulder. "Why the long face, old buddy? So the little lady DA's spooked. Maybe somethin', maybe nothin'. Why should you care?"

"Because it could screw everything up."

"How so?"

"How's a mistrial hit you?"

Tolliver frowned. "I don't think I would like that. Look like somebody's trying to pull something from our side, and it would keep this rotten case alive and in the papers. No, I wouldn't like it at all. You think that's possible?"

Tolliver was bright enough, all right. "Way the judge is acting. He may look old and feeble, but he acts like a judge. And he doesn't like how she's handling the case lately."

"Well, shit..."

"Answer this. If you've such a tight-knit operation, then who the hell was leaking to Savage?"

"Oh, yes, I read about your 'mysterious informant.' Well, not from here, not my people. Way I figure it, from what I know about Savage—cheap, small-time nose-picker, Savage was—it's got to be more along the order of a street scam. Small brain, small attitudes. A little here, a little there, paid a little out, maybe got a little in. What he got was interesting to some people, even got a few do-gooders, but he never got anything a grand jury could pull an indictment from. Except by dyin' the way he did, which got ole Braden indicted, and that was the wrong man."

Nick chuckled in spite of himself. But it sounded right.

"I'll walk you on over to your car. I gotta get back to business. Course, you're welcome to stick around..."

"No thanks. We both have to attend to business."

They strolled along, Tolliver scuffing dirt with heavy steps. "So how's my boy? Much as I could tell on TV, he looked a mite peaked after court yesterday."

"Your million-dollar baby? He's hanging in. He knows it's a tough case. Tell me something, Tolliver. What makes him worth all that bread? You afraid if you didn't go to bat for him in a big way he'd turn state's evidence?"

"If I thought that," Tolliver said matter-of-factly, "I could buy me an icepick, counselor. I could buy me a man to use the icepick. I could buy me a second man to hold Braden while the icepick man run it into one ear and out the other. Then I could pay for the funeral and even be generous to the widow. I could do all that for maybe a hundred grand, and be done with it. So why would I spring with a million for you—which ain't exactly a sure bet, way you been talkin'?"

"Yeah, why?"

"In an average week, Alonzo Braden saves this organization that much in tax loopholes."

Nick's dust-caked car was surrounded by Cadillacs, Lincolns, Porsches, and a couple of Rolls-Royces.

"What's this?" Tolliver looked curiously at Nick's car. "Man like you rents an everyday Chevrolet?"

"I'm eccentric."

"Well, you oughtn't to miss out on life's great pleasures."

"I try not to."

Nick rang the doorbell. At every turn, this case seemed to draw him deeper into unorthodox behavior.

It wasn't that he minded cloak-and-dagger action—he always thought he would have made a great undercover cop—what he minded was that it wasn't getting him anywhere. He felt as if he were sinking deeper and deeper into a bog.

Anne answered the door. She was in robe and nightgown.

"It wasn't Tolliver," Nick said dryly.

She blinked quickly, didn't smile.

"You didn't wait after court. I still want to talk."

"What wasn't Tolliver?" she asked, showing nothing.

"May I come in?"

She stepped aside silently to let him pass, closed the door behind him, and stood right there, as if ready to open it again any second.

Nick took a few steps into the room, his back to her. Soft rock music came from the playroom—much more subdued than the last time. "Let's not play games, okay? I figure somebody's trying to put the arm on you about this case, that's why you're so distracted in court."

"Whatever gave you that—"

"I'm not new at this, okay? I've seen it before. So have you. It's probably happened to you before. It's happened to me. A phone call or two. First I figured Tolliver. So did you. That's why you thought I knew what was going on. But he told me the pressure wasn't coming from him or anyone in his outfit, and he gave me intelligent reasons, the right reasons, why it wouldn't have come from him." He turned to look at her, eyebrows arched.

"Whatever you think," she said coolly, "it's nothing I can't handle."

"Whatever I think..." He was standing next to

Anne's desk. The light was on over it, brochures and travel booklets were spread out. One brochure was next to a half-filled-out application. That, then, was what she had been doing when he came to the door. "Yeah, whatever I think. It's a long drive back from Tolliver's *rancho* kingdom. It was either listen to country-and-western, or think. I thought." He was aware of her sense of privacy, but as he looked obviously at the papers on her desk, she made no move, said nothing.

He casually picked up the brochure next to the application. It advertised an exclusive girls' school— *L'Ecole du Ste. Marie, Berne, Switzerland.* He glanced back at her. "Want to know what I thought about? I thought about an honest, ambitious young assistant DA too feisty to knuckle under to intimidation, to threats."

She put her hand to her throat, fingering the fine gold choker she was wearing.

He looked at the brochure. "I thought about how much this trial could mean to her career." He tossed the brochure down on the desk and turned to her, leaning back against the desk, folding his arms. He let his voice harden. "I've watched you in court, Gronouski. You know your way around the block. With your moxie, first phone call you got like that, you'd have gone to your boss. Right away, either you'd be off the case or there'd be a cordon of cops staked outside this house, or both. That didn't happen. But it's been showing in the courtroom. So you didn't go to Whedon. Nothing you can't handle? So you have been keeping it to yourself. But it shows. Like flashing red lights at an accident, and even the judge is rubber-necking. So what is it?"

"It's personal," she said stiffly, as if he were prying

into her social life. She avoided his eyes.

"Personal? How about *professional?*" Nick was looking grim, feeling grim. "For both of us. This case is important to me in ways you might find hard to believe. Both of us—it's *our* case you're sabotaging!"

"I'm not sabotaging anything." She tried to remain cool, but her hands were clenched.

"Hell you're not. You're not prosecuting this case, Anne, your mind is not in that courtroom. How long do you think it'll be before that sweet old judge steps in and bounces you out on your ass? He isn't happy with you, Miss Prosecutor, and take it from me, that little old man will blow soon, and blow our case away at the same time!"

"I'm doing the best I can!" She raised her fists in front of her.

"Under the circumstances."

"Yes"—she sagged, put a hand over her eyes—"under the circumstances."

"And the circumstances are . . . that message." The recollection suddenly struck him. "That message you got a couple days ago, that was the start of it!"

"What message?" She looked frightened.

"During court, the cop came in and handed you a note. Then right away you asked for a recess. Yeah, I saw you change your face . . ."

"All right." She closed her eyes, tears crept out beneath the lids. "All right. But it's not me, not exactly me . . ."

"Not you?"

"It's Jill. My daughter. It's about her. I can't . . ." She broke into sobs. "I'm so tired, Nick."

"Okay, okay." Nick was stunned. Jill, Jesus. He went to her, took her by the shoulders, then hugged her. "Okay, baby, don't be afraid of me, now. You have to trust me, and I can't even tell you why. You have to let me in, so I can help. I won't let them do it, Anne. I won't let them get at this case, I won't let them get at you."

He steered her to the sofa and helped her sit down. "Now, I'm going to make us a couple of drinks—we never got to that last time around. And we're going to talk. Okay?" He put his hand under her chin and gently tilted her face up. "Okay?"

She nodded.

He went to the bar. He couldn't wait to get the story, to hear a name. He wanted a name. If it was Tolliver, he'd go after him. He would still protect Braden, but he would pin that big mobster right to the wall. There were ways...

From the corner, next to the drapes that were pulled closed for this occasion, he could see Langley seated at his desk—Assistant U.S. Attorney Douglas Langley—and he could see the door.

When the knock came, Langley calmly said, "Come in."

Bill Rossetti opened the door and stuck his head in. "You wanted to see me, sir?"

"He didn't," Nick said, stepping forward, "I do. Close the door."

Rossetti gasped, then quietly closed the door behind him. He looked from Nick to Langley and back. "Are you sure this is wise, Nick, your coming here?"

Langley spoke, all business. "Mr. Hellinger has made a serious accusation, Bill. I wanted you to hear it, and answer it."

"I don't understand."

"You don't?" Nick gave him a sardonic smile. "Well, Rossetti, let me spell it out for you. A few days ago, the Houston Narcotics Squad, tipped by an agent of the U.S. Treasury Department, made a little raid. On some kids. Among those scooped up was a teenager named Jill Gronouski. Ring a bell? I mention this because, you see, owing to some influential and humane connections nobody got booked—officially. But word got to you, didn't it, Rossetti? From your buddy at the Treasury Department."

"That's crazy, why would—"

"We haven't got to the best part yet, have we, Rossetti? The best part is that some scum has been calling Anne Gronouski, threatening to expose her daughter's drug bust and the subsequent failure to book unless she agrees to botch the state's case against Alonzo Braden. And the best part of the best part is just who that scum might be." Nick lifted the telephone receiver and tapped out a number on the pushbuttons.

"Crazy, this is all crazy!" Rossetti slapped his forehead.

"Yeah? Just for the hell of it, why don't you get on this phone and see if she recognizes your voice?"

Anne's distinct, "Hello? Hello?" came from the receiver, which Nick held out to Rossetti.

Rossetti recoiled from the black implement as if it were a cobra. "All right, all right," he whispered frantically, "I called her . . ."

Nick put the phone to his mouth. "It's me, Anne, relax. I just hit paydirt. Get back to you in a minute." He hung up, leaving his hand on the phone and squeezing it under his white knuckles as he fixed his cold eyes on Rossetti.

"But I didn't threaten her," Rossetti said plaintively. "I didn't. I only suggested that victory in this case would give her a certain state-wide prominence, and that her personal life, her family life, might become a lot more public."

"Oh, I beg your pardon, is that all?" Nick dipped his head in mock apology. "I just didn't realize that such a decent message would require several phone calls, several *anonymous* phone calls. Otherwise I might have thought you were trying to blackmail the lady."

"Blackmail! Jesus, Hellinger, what the hell do you think I am?"

"Scum, I believe, was the word I used."

"Bill, for God's sake," Langley broke in, "what were you thinking of?"

"Of Braden, sir." Rossetti leaned across Langley's desk, as if to confide. "Everything he's gone through, what he's done for us, what we need... I wanted to make damn sure he got through this trial free and clear, because—"

"Free and clear?" Nick leaned beside him shoulder to shoulder. "A mistrial? More publicity? Public outcry? Almost certain retrial?"

"I just thought if we could get the case thrown out now, Braden would be free to wrap things up, we'd make our case in Washington against Tolliver—"

"And leave Braden still facing a charge of murder when you guys were finished with him!"

"We would have figured a way to—"

"Meanwhile, make *me* the patsy!" Nick heated up. "Ruin the career of a very valuable and promising young assistant DA—all this would be for the good of the people!"

"If you like," Rossetti said self-righteously.

"I love it! Ends and means. Up to and including derailing the opposition—never mind guilt or innocence—under the banner of God and country!" Nick's voice was hard.

"Hellinger," Rossetti said softly, squaring his shoulders, "you're dangerously naive."

"Right!" Nick slapped the desk and spun away. "I'm a little goody-two-shoes having a mad, blind affair with the legal system."

"Yes, in fact, maybe so."

"Yeah. And let me tell you, after twenty some years in this business, dealing with crooks and cops and crooked feds like you and straight feds and nuts and kooks and all the rest—the rest including, incidentally, a lot of good, simple people fighting for their lives and homes and kids and human rights—I am still naive enough to love our quaint little legal system!"

"Okay." Langley raised a hand. "I've heard enough."

"Sir, there is clear justification for all my actions—"

"I said that's enough!" Langley lowered his head and squeezed his eyebrows together with his fingers. Then he looked up. "Bill, you're relieved of your assignment, effective immediately. I'll be in touch with the Attorney General as soon as Mr. Hellinger leaves. You're excused."

"But I—"

"I said you're excused!"

Rossetti stiffened, turned sharply as a soldier, and marched out.

"I'm sorry." Langley stared at his desktop. "I just—"

"Hold it." Nick was dialing the phone. "Anne? Nick. You won't be receiving any more of those phone calls. Don't ask any questions. Just put it all behind you. Go back to work. As they say, I'll see you in court." He hung up. "Mr. Langley, you were saying?"

Langley rose and circled the desk, turning up his palms apologetically. "I can't tell you how sorry I am. But at least I'm glad we've cleared this up. We don't have many Bill Rossettis, Mr. Hellinger. When we find them, we know what to do with them."

"Well, I'm certainly glad I could bring him to your attention." He walked to the door, then turned. "That was a nice little speech, Langley. Makes my heart beat faster. I've become a little prouder of my country."

"Surely you can see that none of this was *my* doing."

"Oh, sure, I can see that. Harry Hustle there is running around putting his sleazy arm on the assistant DA without so much as a nod to the guy he works for."

Langley looked very disturbed. "You have to believe that I had absolutely nothing to do with this, no knowledge of it at all!"

"Okay. Either way. Either you're bad or blind. Doesn't make any difference."

"But we still have to cooperate on—"

"Listen to me, Langley, and listen good. I'm going to break this case somehow. Me." Nick thumped his chest with his thumb. "And from here on out, you and your flunkies better stay the hell out of my way."

The hotel office suite was thick with Braden's cigarette smoke. Nick sipped his scotch, Braden tipped up his beer bottle for a good slug. Andy toyed with his coffee cup. They sat waiting silently while the busboy cleared away their dinner dishes from the table, loaded his cart, and wheeled it out.

"Man, I'm tired," Andy groaned.

"Now that we've all been alerted to your condition," Nick grumbled, "let's get back to work." He removed the towels that covered the piles of paperwork, photos, and notepads, and spread the documents around the table again.

For a minute they all stared mutely at the mélange. Then Nick said, "Shelldrake's absolutely *positive?*"

Andy nodded. "Nine names, nine airtight alibis. And I mean Shelldrake *checked* them. Wait until you get his bill."

"Yeah, I hope it's steep. I'd like to take it out of Tolliver's goddamn *hide*." Nick reached into his pocket and took out the shamrock and flipped it a few times, listening to it pat back into his palm. "So we're back once again to Savage's informant. We've got to figure he's a possibility."

"Mmm," Andy agreed.

Braden reached under his shirt to scratch his damp chest. Nerves had made him itchy. "You mean as a suspect?"

"If for no other reason than that he's the missing link."

"But why would he—"

"Take the tape?"

"Yeah."

"Same reason as the others—whatever Savage had on that tape."

"But what I'm saying, Nick, is that if what was on the tape was stuff from the informant himself, why would he suddenly turn around and snatch the tape? I mean, he wouldn't be giving information on *himself*."

Nick held the shamrock up and turned it slowly on its rim between his thumb and forefinger, as if examining it for flaws. "Two things are on that tape.

Information and voice. Whoever took that tape wanted to conceal either the information or the voice or both."

"But Shelldrake already checked out the tapes with voices on them other than Savage's, and they have alibis."

"So none of them was the informant."

"Well, it doesn't seem likely to me that the informant would suddenly want to eliminate the information he gave, not badly enough to kill. More likely he would just tell Savage that the information was wrong or something."

"I agree. That leaves the voice."

"But if his voice wasn't on any of the others—and we guess it wasn't since they've been checked out— why would it suddenly be on this last one?"

Nick shrugged. "Maybe some kind of squeeze was being put on."

"All of a sudden?"

"That's the way squeeze plays happen, Lon, all of a sudden. You don't run it up the flagpole to announce a squeeze is coming up. Hey, you know how this stuff works. You're sounding as tired as Andy."

"We been here a long time."

"Look, Braden, you're not under arrest here. You're running out of gas, you can leave. It's your life we're worried about."

"Sorry. I'm okay."

"Andy, you don't do coffee, right?"

"Right." Andy smiled.

"Pour us a round of coffee." While he did, Nick folded his hands behind his head and stared at the ceiling. "From Savage's home, how far's the nearest bus stop?"

"Me?" Braden asked.

"Jesus Christ, anybody in the class can answer."

"In that neighborhood, a mile at least. Buses don't have a route in there. Why?"

"You said that when the taxi dropped you, the street was deserted. So how did the killer get there?"

"Maybe by cab, same as me."

"I don't think the guy, especially if he was the informant, would risk having a taxi take him there. But anyway, how did he leave? And if he came and went by a car he drove himself, why wasn't it parked out in front?"

"He was afraid," Andy volunteered. "Once the crime was discovered, somebody might remember his car."

Nick shook his head. "The murder wasn't premeditated. Savage had a gun, the guy used a poker. That's what's called your basic spur-of-the-moment situation."

They sat musing.

Nick rubbed his head. "There's something we're overlooking. Got to be something right in front of our eyes."

"Why you think that, Nick?" Andy asked innocently.

"Because we're not coming up with anything new, so I just decided, that's why. It's a command decision."

"Oh."

Nick rearranged the photos on the table in front of them, like pieces of a puzzle, changing perspectives that might jar new visions. "Lon, you were there when they took these pictures. Is there anything the camera missed?"

"Me? I wasn't there."

"Hunh?" Nick peered at him.

"How would I be there? I was down at the station being booked."

Nick blinked at him. Then he jammed his finger down on one photo and drew it over in front of Braden. It was the photo of the floor scene that included the lower legs of three men, two in police trousers and one wearing street pants, all three sets of pants legs water-splotched. Nick circled the legs in the street clothes with his finger. "This isn't *you?*"

"Nope."

"Then who the hell *is* it?"

Braden and Andy leaned close to scrutinize the photo. Nick straightened up from his chair, almost knocking it over, and stalked over to the window and looked out at the city lights.

"Well," Braden said, "I got wet in the sprinklers, and the two cops that arrested me, they got wet. That's three."

"The killer," Nick turned to face them, leaning back with the heels of his hands on the windowsill, "makes four."

CHAPTER 10

EARLY MORNING of an already humid day, and the joggers were sweating in the park. Vanity kept Nick wearing his warm-up suit instead of running in shorts; regular joggers' legs were so goddamn lean, and Nick's made him look like a bricklayer. Plus his stomach was not quite back to fighting trim. But he didn't care. He wanted the sweat to pour out of him in buckets. It was cleansing, refreshing and draining. The same way his brain felt after the exhaustion of the night before when, finally, the odd facts and recollections began to flow together from the agonizing marathon of thinking.

Yes, even the last time out here in the park had produced a bit of information that turned out to be crucial. And when Nick needed to put the whole thing together, he had remembered it. So last night he had been able to give Andy a relatively simple job to do: find out if Savage had an automatic sprinkler system, and if he did, what time it operated.

And here came Andy, pedaling ferociously on his bicycle. Nick smiled through the sweat that dribbled over his eyes and mouth. Andy was moving with the pace of news.

He skidded to a stop and jumped off the bike, but before he could speak, Nick said, "Why the hell are you wearing an Astros cap? As a diehard Phillies fan, I consider that gross insubordination."

"How can you joke"—Andy puffed—"at a time like this?"

"Who's joking? What've you got?"

"First let me ask you a question. Besides the water on the pants, what got you thinking like that?"

"Tolliver."

"Tolliver? But he's not—"

"Tolliver gave me a brief personal assessment of Savage's operation—and whatever else you may think, he's not dumb about what makes people tick. And something he said stuck in this fertile brain of mine, something about a street scam, a little here, a little there."

"I don't follow you."

"Just give."

"You're gonna love it!"

"Yeah, yeah, along with the birds and bees. Just give."

Nick walked and Andy wheeled his bike alongside. "Those legs you thought were Braden's, in the photo? They're Detective Donovan's! And there *is* an automatic timer. The sprinklers were programmed to shut off at nine p.m. Donovan didn't arrive until nine-fifteen!"

"Mmm."

"Wait, it gets even better!"

"I'm not sure my heart can stand the excitement."

"Shelldrake managed to check the police log—or he got somebody to do it, he wouldn't tell me. Donovan was on his dinner break when Savage was killed—but he didn't go to dinner!"

"Oh? Shelldrake managed to get his stomach pumped?"

"I mean, at least Donovan didn't eat at the place where he's been eating every night for the past four years!"

"My, my"—Nick grinned evilly—"such a man of habits."

"So that means—"

"What things mean, you don't have to tell me. Facts are what I counted on you for."

Andy sagged. "You mean I didn't—"

"You did super." Nick grabbed his arm and pulled him to a stop and peered into his eager face. "Kid, no matter what anyone tells you, winning is more fun than losing."

"Hellinger's Law?" Andy asked, beaming.

"George Armstrong Custer's."

Tolliver shook his head doubtfully. "Man, I don't know about direct personal involvement." He sat on the top rail of the fence and looked glumly down at his big hands draped between his knees. Near him, a solitary steer gazed curiously out at Nick, as if the steer knew Nick didn't belong there. "It isn't my style. Makes me nervous."

"It is your personal involvement that would give

it credibility." Nick stuck a long piece of grass between his teeth. "You're going to have plenty to be nervous about if your boy gets convicted. And don't give me any nonsense about what kind of money he saves you by working on the books. The real worry is, guy faces life in prison, that may be reason enough for him to turn."

Tolliver snapped his head up. "Braden wouldn't do that. I know him too well."

Nick shrugged. "People have been known to take on whole new cooperative personalities once that gavel drops for the last time. Yeah, I think Braden's tough too, but if it comes down to your life or his, I'd give it even money. And that's me. If I were you, I wouldn't want to bet on it at all."

Tolliver thought for a while, looking out over the vast rolling land that was his. "You could be settin' me up."

"Oh, sure, what a brilliant idea. For what? You kill Savage? If you did, I wish you'd have told me a long time ago. I would've played my defense a little differently."

"Course I didn't."

"Then let's cut the trash, Tolliver. We're not children. You spent a lot of money and trusted me this far. You tell me I'm making sense with what I've figured out. You want the job done, I'm telling you how. I want to win this case, and I'm willing to put myself on the hot seat with you. I have two choices. I can try it alone, or I can walk away from the whole damn thing. I already have my money."

"You think I'm scared to do it?"

"You're talking like a kid before his first roller-coaster ride."

"I haven't been scared since the first time I rode a bull."

"Worried, scared, whatever. All I know is, we're going to do it or not, and I haven't got much time."

Tolliver nodded. He dropped down from the fence, his brows knitted in concentration. He strolled along the fence to where the steer was nosing out, and casually swatted the big snout, causing the steer to yank its heavy head away and amble off.

Nick leaned against the fence and watched him, chewing on a stalk of grass.

Tolliver turned and cocked his head. "You're pretty sure this'll work."

"Depends on how good an actor you can be. Best way to be an actor is to make yourself believe what you're saying."

Tolliver raised his eyebrows. "Be willing to actually go through with it."

"For my part, I won't be bluffing. I'll mean everything I say. And it'll make it easier for me if it doesn't sound like you're bluffing either—even to me."

Tolliver peered at him, then nodded slowly. "Let's set it up."

"Fine." They started to walk away together. "And Tolliver, one thing."

"Name it."

"After this little scene is played, I don't want to hear from you again. I don't want to hear from anybody working for you. I did my job. This is a one-time-only show."

"I got you."

"Vice versa, I'm sure."

Everyone in the courtroom rose, the judge took his seat at precisely ten a.m. He sat down, everyone sat down.

He nodded to both counsel tables, then said, "Mr. Hellinger?"

"Your Honor, before resuming, I wonder if I might approach the bench."

"Certainly, counselor."

The judge leaned over to hear Nick's whispered message, nodded, and leaned back. "Miss Gronouski? Would you join us, please?"

Nick watched her, she did not look at him. He figured at best she was now ambivalent about him. She did not stand close to him before the bench.

The judge leaned forward again. "Mr. Hellinger has requested a twenty-four-hour recess, Miss Gronouski. He suggests that some new evidence has come to light that could dramatically affect the trial, and wishes time to develop that evidence. Will the prosecution join in the motion?"

She hesitated, looked off, then answered in a flat voice, "It will, Your Honor."

"Thank you," Nick said to her as she turned away.

The judge banged his gavel. "The court will stand in recess until this same time tomorrow."

Braden stood waiting in bemusement as Nick returned to the table. "What's going on?" he asked urgently.

"Better you shouldn't know, Lon. But it's all in your favor. Andy, get moving."

Andy quickly gathered up his papers and left.

"But, Nick," Braden persisted, "you can't leave me in the dark now."

"Yes I can. If somebody should ask you about what's coming down now, I don't want you to have to lie. So I don't want you to know. If this works, my job will be finished. But you still have a tough road ahead of you that doesn't even relate to this trial, right? Concentrate on that."

"Christ, I almost forgot."

"That's what I mean. Why don't you get on out of here, courtrooms are depressing."

He stopped Anne as she was leaving. "This won't reflect badly on you, Miss Prosecutor."

"Oh, really?" She barely glanced at him.

"Really."

"Well, how nice." She started away, then stopped and turned to him, putting one hand on her hip. "Mr. Hellinger, I suppose I should be grateful for . . . certain things you've done. And I guess I am. You've got some kind of sensational new evidence that'll turn this case, that's fine. All's fair and all that . . ."

"It has nothing to do with technicalities or cheap tricks, Anne, it'll be justice."

"Sure, okay, I'll buy that. I happen to believe in justice, even if it means I lose a case. But you know an awful lot about me and my private life now. And it doesn't seem like justice to me that you won't tell me who it was that was threatening me, and why."

"I can't."

"Well . . ." She shrugged.

He took her arm, which tensed at his touch. "I mean really, Anne. No games. Sure, I did what I did to protect the case, but I also did it for you—for you as in Anne Gronouski, not as in prosecutor. Some day maybe you'll know. But it can't come from me."

"Attorney-client relationship?"

"Beyond that."

She smirked. "The defendant's *extended family*, then, if you get my drift."

"I get your drift. Beyond that too." He shouldn't have added that—a little loose-tongued. But at least her eyes softened.

She nodded, accepting. She simply said, "Okay," and left.

• • ○

Andy was on the phone when Nick walked into the office suite. He nodded at Nick and continued. "No, I'm afraid Mr. Hellinger hasn't returned yet . . . No, I haven't heard from him since your last call. But the moment I do, I'll see that he gets your message, I'll pass it on to him personally . . . Absolutely, I understand . . . Right. Good-bye."

"Didn't take long," Nick said, slipping off his coat and loosening his tie.

"That's the fifth time he's phoned. You can almost hear the sweat dripping off him."

"Good. Christ, it's hot."

"Cool in here."

"Hot in here, don't contradict me."

"Well, the air-conditioning is on." Andy returned to the newspaper crossword puzzle. "Lot cooler in Philadelphia, hunh?"

"Hot in Philadelphia too. I should be practicing in Minnesota."

"Think you could become a Twins fan?"

"Vikings." Nick stripped off his sodden shirt.

Andy looked up. "I didn't know you were a football fan. How come not the Eagles?"

"The Eagles never win anything."

"The Phillies have been dry longer than—"

"Hey, do I have to explain everything?"

"Nope." Andy turned serious. "I hope you don't think I'm taking any of this lightly, Nick. I'm worried. Nervous conversation . . ."

"I'm worried enough for both of us. Plus I'm paid for worrying. You're not. Do the puzzle, answer the phone. I'm going to take a shower." He strolled to the bathroom, saying over his shoulder, "And, Andy?

Be a sweetheart, make me a cup of coffee, hunh?"

He spent several minutes in the shower. He felt as if he still had Tolliver's ranch dirt to scrub out of his pores. Over the stream of water, he vaguely heard the tinkle of the telephone, and smiled.

He toweled off, went into the bedroom, and put on a fresh suit of clothes, then returned to the main room.

"He called again," Andy said.

"Yeah." He sat down, stretched, yawned, sipped his coffee, checked his pocket watch. "Almost time to go."

"Forgive me for asking, but . . ."

"Ask."

"You going to be carrying . . . a gun?"

"You think I'm Wyatt Earp? Don't be crazy, kid. Carrying a gun is the best way to get yourself shot."

"I just thought—"

"You watch too many movies. This is just a nice, simple get-together among us law-abiding citizens." He got up, stretched again, straightened his tie, and headed for the door. "Keep up the good work, kid. Talk to you later."

"Good luck."

"Luck I got." He bounced the shamrock in his palm. "Ta-ta."

Shelldrake did neat work, all right. Nobody could tell he'd ever been there. His directions, passed through Andy, on how to approach the rear from another street without being seen were as precise as a blueprint. Anybody who checked the rear French doors a while ago would have found them locked; Nick followed his instructions and the doors opened like magic. Savage's study had been cleaned up by police personnel or friends or the caretaker and the curtains were closed.

Shelldrake's a very good man, love to have him in Philadelphia, Nick mused. But years went into such knowledge of an area, of contacts, of methods appropriate to the place, and this was Shelldrake's turf. Nick was impressed by the fact that even Andy, who had worked with him, didn't know *how* he worked. Very good man.

As far as the other people involved in this little drama, Nick hoped all of them would perform well.

He sat down at the desk, picked up the phone, and dialed.

It was answered on the second ring. "Homicide, Sergeant Becker."

"Detective Donovan, please? My name is Hellinger."

"Hold on." Becker's more distant voice called, "Roy? It's that lawyer, Hellinger. Pick up on three."

There was a click, another voice: "I got it, Jeff." The next click indicated that Becker had hung up. "Mr. Hellinger? Roy Donovan." Donovan's voice was low and close, as if he were cupping his hand around the receiver for privacy.

"Understand you've been trying to reach me."

"Yeah, I have."

"Sorry I've been out."

"No problem, no problem. What I was interested in was, well, when you sprung that surprise recess in court this morning, I, unh, well naturally I checked with the DA's office, and, unh, it sounded like maybe you had a handle on something we might be interested in."

"Just defending my client."

"Well . . . remember that conversation we had?

About how, if there was anything you found that would be a new lead on something, you know? I mean, we made the arrest and all, and for my money we got the right guy. But I'm as interested as anybody else in the truth, and remember I said I'd follow up on anything you might uncover. Personally. Remember?"

"Yeah."

"So, unh..."

"I'm glad you brought that up, Roy. As a matter of fact, I *could* use some help. You know I believe my client to be innocent."

"I know."

"Well, I might be onto something that would lead in another direction. I'd get a court order, but that'd take time. On the other hand, I'd hate to get arrested for breaking and entering..."

"Listen, whatever it is, I'm willing to help. Let's get this thing tied up."

Nick let a long, silent moment go by, as if considering whether to give Donovan the information. Donovan was nicely anxious. "Okay, Roy, it's that tape. That missing tape."

"I know what you mean, the one you thought the killer had taken, from that empty box in the photograph."

"That's it."

"You found it?"

Nick smiled but didn't let that get into his voice. "Not exactly. But it turns out that Savage kept a set of duplicates."

"Duplicates!" Donovan echoed breathlessly.

"I managed to get a line on a carpenter who claims he built a secret storage place in Savage's study."

"No kidding. Imagine that."

Nick could hear the dryness in Donovan's voice. "I'm with the guy now. In Apple Springs. It'll take me a good two hours to make it back to Houston. If you could meet me at the Savage house at, say, eight-thirty . . ."

"Eight-thirty's fine."

"Because, you know, with you on the scene, nobody could accuse me of pulling a fast one."

"I understand."

"You can also understand, I hope, that I'd like this to be just between you and me, okay? Until we know what we've got."

"You and me, that's it."

"I can't tell you how much I appreciate this."

"Part of my job, to get at the truth. Eight-thirty, I'll be there. Count on it."

"I am counting on it, Roy. I really am."

Nick hung up and leaned back, grinning at the phone—baring his teeth like a dog. He checked his watch. Six-oh-nine. Perfect. Donovan could say he was going on his dinner break. Nick figured twenty minutes.

He would savor those twenty minutes in complete silence. That was his ground rule for the operation; from the time he picked up the phone to call Donovan, he would not be disturbed for any reason—unless somehow it hadn't worked with Donovan, in which case he would have to change the plan. But it had worked. So he would sit in silence and watch the twilight fade into darkness behind the closed drapes and concentrate on establishing control over his mind.

It was not so different from when he would go into court. His exercise was not just to review, but to consolidate his thoughts, trim his mind for mental combat. It was a kind of meditation that often gave him the edge. He willed himself to be fully confident, totally focused, tightly controlled.

The street was deserted. A dog barked three times perhaps a quarter of a mile away. Crickets in the woods behind the house sounded like a chorus of fine, small ratchets. Another sound joined them: the rhythmic squish-slap of the automatically timed rainbirds in the backyard.

Outside, the light was now gone. Nick flicked his cigarette lighter to see his pocket watch: six-twenty-seven. He snapped the watch shut and put that and the lighter back in his pocket.

He saw the beams of headlights reaching up the street before he heard the car. The car passed the house without slowing. The beams bent around the corner of the next intersection. He listened intensely, heard the engine shut off.

He counted the seconds. Eighty-three of them before the crickets suddenly hushed. Now just the rainbirds. Then soft sloshy footfalls on the lawn to the French doors. A key slid into the lock. The doors wheezed open, momentarily raising the volume of the rainbirds, then closed. Now a man's breathing in the study.

"A little early, aren't you, Roy?" Nick switched on the desk lamp.

Donovan's startled eyes turned to the light. His hand went quickly inside his jacket.

"You're running up one hell of a cleaning bill"—Nick eyed the splotched bottoms of his trouser legs—"you know that?"

Donovan dropped his hand from his coat, let his eyelids fall to normal position. "What're you doing here, Nick? You said eight-thirty."

Nick appreciated Donovan's attempt at innocence. "I lied."

"Why?"

"I sometimes do."

"You could've been sitting here another couple of hours, if I hadn't been able to break away early. By yourself. I assume you're alone."

"I assume you are too. We can't afford to have anybody else involved, can we?"

Donovan didn't answer. His eyes flitted around the room.

"In case you're wondering, I parked around the corner, same as you did."

"Oh? I didn't see—"

"Different corner. But I mean, same as you did, I assume, the times you met with Savage."

"The times I *what?*"

Cops made great liars. But Donovan's eyes gave him away.

"You couldn't park very near the house," Nick went on, "because some neighborhood kid might have picked up on the car—we know how they love to spot unmarked cop cars—and told his parents that Savage was being regularly visited by a cop. That would have been bad for business, am I right?"

Donovan's face twisted into a sneer. "What is this? I park around the corner, you make a story out of it. You're looking for a patsy."

"Oh, no. It may sound quaint, but I'm looking for the truth. I think I've found it. Savage's information wasn't coming from inside the organization, he was getting it off the street. But *how?*" Nick rubbed his chin.

Donovan stood sneering, stoop-shouldered, one eye drooping, feet planted apart, arms loose at his sides.

"As a well-known TV personality, he had too high a profile to go poking around the flotsam and jetsam of Houston's underworld. And he operated alone, didn't employ a team of snoopers and diggers—didn't trust anybody, in fact. But he had to rely on *somebody* else who might have access to the areas he was so interested in. Now, a plainclothes cop would be well connected, with a network of snitches at his disposal. He could get information from *anywhere*, couldn't he, Roy? And a *detective*, why he even could get a line inside the *mob*, maybe."

"Anybody could pick up that theory, Hellinger, that's no mystery. But if you're thinking it's me, you're crazy."

"Am I?" Nick leaned forward on his elbows and toyed with the shamrock between his hands. "Last fall, to celebrate your promotion to sergeant, you took a flier on some mutual funds. It proved disastrous, left you deep in debt. Paul Savage bailed you out."

"Like hell he did."

"Well, yes and no. Bank records showing Savage's checks made out to cash, deposits to your account in the same amounts always just a day or so after. See"— Nick smiled icily—"I've got a snitch of my own. Surprised? Very good man. But those amounts from Savage, they were never enough to bail you out. So you went to the loan sharks. You put the squeeze on Savage for more bread to pay off the sharks. He refused, you got nasty. I would be guessing now, wouldn't I, except for that tape?"

"Every word here is a guess, and a bad one at that."

"When you started pushing for more money, he started taping you. That made that last tape of his, the missing one, very important. You wanted it, he refused, he pulled a gun, you were quicker with the poker. Smart too, if you'll accept the compliment,

207

for not using your own gun, which would have been traceable. I am guessing a bit on the final moments, of course. But a duplicate of that tape, made on another hidden machine, would bring us very close indeed to the final—"

"Shut up a minute!" Donovan snarled, like somebody trying to cool an argument.

But what Donovan was expressing was his sudden need to think. He fidgeted, rubbed his face, scratched his neck, shifted his feet, blinked his eyes. He started to speak, then stopped. He breathed as if he had just run a mile. Gradually he calmed himself, arriving, apparently, at the realization that further argument in light of the facts was pointless.

"Tell me, Hellinger," he said huskily, "we're a couple of pretty bright guys in this business, I was pretty careful—how'd you tumble?"

"Not easy, Roy, not easy. You played it pretty good. But this . . ." He slid the wet-trouser photo out of a manila envelope on the desk and shoved it across. "Look at your trousers, Roy, then look at this photo. The sprinklers were off by the time you reported arriving at the crime scene, but they were on when you left Savage earlier—just as they're on now."

Donovan studied the photo. "Pretty minor point," he grumbled. "Not much to give you a run at. So you must be pretty damn smart, Hellinger."

Nick shrugged. "I try."

"Damned lucky."

"I am lucky."

Donovan spread his hands on the desk and leaned on straight arms. "Smart enough to be wired, right?"

"Right." He took from his inside jacket pocket a tiny battery-powered tape recorder, which was running.

Donovan nodded, his cheek twitching. "And there

aren't any duplicate tapes. That was just to get me here."

"Right again."

"You lie sometimes."

"Yeah."

"Okay, you got me here. You're a rotten mouthpiece for the mob, so you want a deal. What you want, Braden out?"

"Yeah."

"Well, right there you ain't so smart. I already testified, and how the hell can I go back on that and have any jury in the world believe me?"

"You can tell the truth."

"What? *What?*" Donovan slapped his forehead in disbelief.

"I said I'm looking for the truth. I wasn't lying about that."

"You mean—"

"All I wanted to do was clear up the case. So now it's cleared up, on tape, the works. No more squeeze. That's it."

"So now what, you expect to just walk out of here?"

"With you."

"You crazy dumb bastard, you are not moving!"

"Figure it this way. You won't beat me hand-to-hand. And you'd be insane to use your service revolver, unless you plan to dig the slugs out of me yourself and scatter them over the ocean like funeral ashes."

"Except you leave me no choice." Donovan reached inside his jacket for the shoulder-holster that held his .38.

"Touch that iron," came a big voice from behind, "you're a dead man!"

Donovan froze for a second, then slowly turned

his head around to see Leo enter from the hallway, a .45 automatic in his hand. Tolliver was right behind him.

"I lied again, Donovan," Nick said calmly, causing Donovan's head to swivel back toward him. "For obvious reasons, I needed backup. All things considered, I could hardly go to your superiors."

"Still a shakedown!" Donovan spouted. "Tolliver and you!"

"Wrong. Just going to take you in. Shall we go?"

"Wait up, counselor." Tolliver stepped in front and held up a hand. "You misled me a little on this here, from what I just heard. I can't sit still for this."

"We had a deal, Tolliver," Nick said sternly.

"We *had* a deal maybe. But not this." He gazed disdainfully down his nose at Donovan. "I have nothing against a cop doing his job, even if that may cause me a little upset from time to time. Now, this bozo cooperating with a newsman is one thing. But bugging up my operation just to pad his own pockets—using his badge as a collection plate—I just can't stomach that. I have a queer kind of moral sense about a crooked cop, if he isn't mine. If we can't depend on straight cops to make it safe for our beautiful Texas daughters to walk the streets, well then . . . No, I draw the line when a cop is crooked *and* tries to get his hooks into me. That cancels our deal, counselor."

"Didn't figure you for a welcher, Tolliver."

"I don't care what you figured, Hellinger. Leo, get this cop outta my sight. Like forever. That lake in the old quarry. And make sure he will never float up."

Leo motioned to Donovan with his .45.

"For chrissake, Tolliver." Nick bounced out of his seat, "Think! What about Braden?"

"What *about* Braden?"

"You want Braden, you must have Donovan. You

have to have them both, man, if you want Braden back!"

"Steers and mares"—Tolliver sighed—"talking about two different things. You've got no proof against Donovan, nothing that'd stand up."

"Why do you think I taped what he—"

"Oh, now, Mr. Hellinger. You know better, but you don't know me. The cassette in your pocket? He'd scream entrapment. I'm a little keen on the law myself, see. And you know I'm right. So where's that leave us? Same old dried-up waterhole. No, I like it the way I decided it now."

"And what the hell am I supposed to use to spring Braden?"

"Oh, counselor, you were smart enough to come up with this here, you're smart enough to come up with something else. Go ahead on, Leo."

"Wait a minute." Nick hurried around the desk. "What if he agreed to cooperate?"

"What? Now, you mean? Oh, sure, and the minute we hand him in, he rolls over on us."

Donovan looked back and forth from Nick to Tolliver, face white and pasty as ricotta cheese, wide eyes streaked and glistening like marbles, mouth wriggling like a dug-up worm.

"How about it, Donovan," Nick asked quickly, "Tolliver's way or mine?"

"It was self-defense!" Donovan blurted, starting to move but freezing at the reminder of Leo's .45. "Savage had a gun on me! He was gonna shoot!"

"That's your story?"

"Truth! I swear!"

Nick patted Donovan's arm and nodded hopefully at Tolliver. "Okay. And Roy, you'll be sure to tell that to your lawyer, right?"

"Right! Right! I'll tell him! Self-defense!"

"What about it, Clint?"

Tolliver thought for a minute. "Okay, Leo, hand me that hogleg and go bring the car around." Donovan slumped into a chair, Tolliver stood over him. "See that you memorize that tune, Mr. Policeman. 'Cause what I didn't do tonight, I can just as well do tomorrow."

"And, Leo," Nick called. "Leo, wave your arm once over your car. That'll signal my backup."

"You got a—"

"Yeah." Nick grinned at the stunned Tolliver. "Man can't be too careful in this business, right?"

"He lies sometimes," Donovan muttered vacantly.

"Well, I'll be."

Yeah, his own backup would bring Nick's own car around. He'd finally get a chance to lay eyes on Manolo Shelldrake.

Morning headlines screamed the news: *"COP CONFESSES TO NEWSCASTER SLAYING! Houston Detective Claims Self-Defense in Killing of Paul Savage"; "ALONZO BRADEN EXPECTED TO BE FREED TODAY"*.

Andy folded the newspaper under his arm as they trotted up the courthouse steps. "You took a hell of a chance! Suppose he'd have blown you away?"

Nick shrugged. "Then you'd have to make the trip to Philadelphia alone."

"What?" Andy stopped.

"I need somebody in my office to make coffee—and maybe be a law associate in the firm of Carroll and Hellinger. I figured you might be available."

Nick continued up the steps. Andy scampered after him, speechless.

The courtroom was filled as usual, but the atmosphere was completely changed. There was a kind of cheerful drama about the place. Alonzo Braden would go free. And those who might be disappointed with the unexpected end of this murder trial could look forward with excitement to the upcoming trial of a cop turned killer. It was all very entertaining, Nick thought.

Not to denigrate the emotion of Braden's family, and his friends who were, unfortunately, few, due to the particular company Braden was obliged to keep, Nick chose not to acknowledge some henchmen seated among the spectators. They could now dare to be present, and they were a happy bunch. They would not be happy for long. The U.S. Attorney's office would see to that. And soon Braden would be free of them, maybe live some kind of normal life and be appreciated for what he had done.

The judge entered, gaveled the court to order. Anne rose and made the pro forma motion, and the judge nodded.

Looking pale and emotionless as ever, the judge made the announcement: "In light of developments made known to the court during the past twenty-four hours, and with the concurrence of the prosecution, the court has no choice but to dismiss all charges against the defendant." He banged the gavel. "Court is adjourned."

The room broke into a general hubbub, above which rose a couple of whoops from Tolliver's crew.

Braden turned quickly to Nick and stuck out his hand. "You know I can't thank you enough, or properly."

Nick held his hand firmly. "I feel thanked enough."

"Well . . ."

"Half-time's over, right? Back to the fray. You've

got guts, my friend. One day we'll all be thanking *you*."

Braden smiled wryly. "It's a living."

"Get out of here, go join your family."

Cara finally broke through the crowd and hurled herself upon her husband, hugging him while she cried. Julie hugged him from the other side.

Nick turned from them to Andy. "Get packed up and get out of here. We'll have plenty of time to talk about all this later. Take the day off. We'll leave tomorrow."

Nick left him abruptly and went over to Anne. "Hey," he said softly, smiling.

"Well, you were right all along—about the murder."

"Yeah, well . . ."

"Shame we have to go back to our opposite sides."

"Maybe not so opposite."

"I'm afraid so, Nick. Maybe someday I'll—what would you call it, mellow? But as long as I can, I'll hold onto my scruples."

"Maybe one day you'll see me differently, maybe even feel like giving me a call."

"Doubt it."

"Maybe one day." He smiled wistfully, sadly trapped in a role he never wanted.

"Anyway"—her bright smile was mechanical—"congratulations on your work."

"Thanks."

On the courthouse steps, the press was surrounding Braden. Tolliver and his cohorts were beaming and back-slapping. At the curb, limousines were waiting—Tolliver's chariots.

Julie broke away and came running up to Nick, carrying a box wrapped in delightfully clumsy style. She thrust it at him. "On account of you kept your promise!" she chirped. "It's a scarf. I knitted it myself. I hope you like purple."

He swept her up in his arms, planted a kiss on her cheek.

"If I write to you will you write to me?" she asked.

"Bet on it, sunshine."

She scampered back to rejoin her family.

Fredericks, the reporter, walked over, notepad in hand. "Well, Mr. Hellinger, Lon Braden isn't a murderer, so he can go back to work for the same old organization." He nodded in the direction of Braden and his family who were being ushered into the Tolliver limousines. "So that means the public got justice, I suppose."

Nick regarded the reporter's sarcastic smile, and looked away. "Justice, my friend, has many faces, injustice as many masks; the wisest judge cannot always tell between them."

"Another Hellinger's Law?"

"Just the truth." Nick watched Anne walk away down the steps. "No big deal."